Incident at Confederate Gulch

When 17-year-old Tom Hogan's sister is offered a job at a theatre in the mining town of Diamond City, Montana, he little realizes that his twin is in danger of being drawn into a life of prostitution. When he discovers the truth, the young man sets off to rescue her.

But his journey leads him into the underground world of gambling dens and hurdy-gurdy houses. His plans go awry and unwittingly he becomes involved in the break-up of a gang of opium smugglers. He also learns that being a real man means a good deal more than just carrying a gun or winning at a Faro table.

Incident at Confederate Gulch

Ethan Harker

A Black Horse Western

ROBERT HALE · LONDON

© Ethan Harker 2014
First published in Great Britain 2014

ISBN 978-0-7198-1298-9

Robert Hale Limited
Clerkenwell House
Clerkenwell Green
London EC1R 0HT

www.halebooks.com

The right of Ethan Harker to be identified as
author of this work has been asserted by him
in accordance with the Copyright, Designs and
Patents Act 1988

Typeset by
Derek Doyle & Associates, Shaw Heath
Printed and bound in Great Britain by
CPI Antony Rowe, Chippenham and Eastbourne

CHAPTER 1

It had been a hard winter and a late spring. Only now, at the end of April, had it proved possible to sow seed and there was no certainty that it would come up. This corner of Montana was bleak and inhospitable and if her husband had not been killed in the war, then Melanie Hogan would probably not have been scraping a living here with her seventeen-year-old son and daughter. The family had moved to the little smallholding in 1860, when the twins were nine. It had only ever been meant for a temporary base, until her husband could get something better suited to his talents. But the war came and Jacob was killed and now, three years after the surrender at Appomattox, she and her children were still struggling to survive here.

They were all three of them sitting outside the house when the stranger rode up. He was a smart one all right: plump, florid and with the sharpest suit of clothes you ever saw a man on horseback wearing. He was even sporting a fancy waistcoat. The rider reined in and swept off his hat in a gallant gesture.

'Ma'am,' said the stranger, in an educated voice which was pleasant to the ear, 'Have I the pleasure of addressing the relict of Jacob Hogan?'

'I'm his widow, if that's what you are asking,' said Melanie shortly.

'I had the privilege of knowing your late husband, ma'am. I promised myself that if ever I was in this neck of the woods, then I would make sure to come by your house.'

'Won't you set and take a drink of water?' said Melanie.

The man dismounted with an easy, flowing grace that was almost feline in its delicacy. He accepted a mug of water and then smiled at the three of them.

'I had no idea that Jacob's children would have grown into such fine young folk.' He turned to Kathleen, who was a raw-boned girl of distinctly homely appearance. 'Why, you are a regular, rustic beauty! Surely you have already been spotted by somebody wanting you to model clothes or act on the stage?'

The flattery was laid on with a trowel, but was none the less effective for that. The plain girl smiled shyly and even her mother allowed her face to relax a little.

'Do I take it that nobody has yet offered you any work in this line?' asked the man, in apparent amazement. He turned to her mother. 'Why, this is an unlooked-for piece of luck for both of us. By an uncanny coincidence, I am currently seeking elegant young ladies such as your daughter, Mrs Hogan.'

'What are we talking of here?' Kathleen's mother asked, a mite suspiciously.

'Why, to begin with, acting on the stage at a theatre in which I have an interest. She need not speak; only wear the necessary costumes and stand there decorously. Later, it might lead to work modelling clothes for some of the big stores with which I have dealings. We shall see.'

Melanie Hogan turned to her daughter and said, 'What do you say to this, Kathleen?'

The girl shrugged her shoulders and said, 'I don't mind.'

Kathleen's brother Tom did not rightly take to the visitor the way his mother and sister did, but so effusive was the fellow that even Melanie Hogan, not noted for being easily gulled, warmed to him after a space. By the time he left it was agreed that he would furnish Kathleen with a set of new clothes and provide her with a ticket from Cooper's Creek, the nearest town, to the impressively named Diamond City, where his theatre was located.

Incredible to relate, so dazzled were they by Mr Ezekiel Granger and his smooth ways that it was not until some time after he had left that any of them recollected that he had not mentioned just what his association with Jacob Hogan had been.

Five weeks later, and a month after Kathleen had gone off to Diamond City, Tom and his ma had still received no word from her; not even to inform them of her safe arrival. Because his mother was growing uneasy Tom offered to walk into Cooper's Creek and find out what was what. Perhaps he would hear some word of Mr Granger there.

Now they say that truth is stranger than fiction and this was certainly the case the day that Tom Hogan fetched up in Cooper's Creek after a five-mile walk from his home, because almost the first words he heard being spoken by two men on the sidewalk touched upon his enquiries.

'Those poor young fools,' said one man to another as Tom came nigh to them. 'A new set of clothes and they'll believe any sort of foolishness.'

'Serve 'em right, say I,' said his companion. 'They're no better than they ought to be, some of them country girls. If they stayed at home, doing what is needful there, they would not be getting themselves into such trouble.' He spat a stream of tobacco juice into the roadway.

At the words *a new set of clothes* a chill hand of fear clutched Tom's heart and he felt emboldened to go up to the men and speak without being introduced.

'Excuse me, sir,' he began. 'Did I hear something about a new set of clothes?'

'You might have done,' said the man. 'If, that is, you were listening in on a private conversation. Why, what's it to you, boy?'

'Why, only this. A flashy kind of fellow calling himself Granger came by our place over a month since. Said he knew my pa, who is dead. Then he offered my sister work in some theatre and she went off. We have not heard since and I am afeared that some harm has befallen her.'

The two men looked at the boy compassionately and seemed a little embarrassed. At length, the man who had spoken to him said, 'Well, some harm might have befallen her, but not perhaps what you mean by the word. There was a man in this here town, trying to get girls to go up to Diamond City to work in places that are, well, not right nice. Some of the fathers round here did not take to him and so he stopped his recruiting in town and went round some farms and such. Mayhap your sister is one of those he persuaded. I'm sorry, son.' He turned away from Tom and began a conversation with his friend which was clearly designed to signal to the boy that they did not wish to talk further to him.

Tom was at a loss to know what step he should take next, then he remembered the old man in the general store, Mr Paxton, and decided to go and consult him. He went to the store, which by a mercy was empty and set the case out as it seemed to him.

Old Mr Paxton shook his head sorrowfully and sighed. 'Truth is, young Tom, I think your sister took a wrong turn when she listened to that smooth-talking scoundrel. He tried to get some of the girls from town to go off with him, but their pas got right contentious about it and if he had not stopped, I don't know but that he might have been tarred and feathered or worse. Look ahere now, I have one of the handbills he was after giving out.' Mr Paxton delved beneath his counter for a few seconds and then pulled out a sheet of paper, upon which was printed the following:

DIAMOND CITY
WANTED: FIFTY WAITER GIRLS!!!
High Wages, Easy Work
Pay in Gold Promptly Every Week
Must Appear in Short Clothes or no
Engagement!
GOOD STEPPERS
Make Yourself Some Money
FUN GALORE!! FINE CLOTHING!!
Nothing Untoward Which Could Tend
To Affect a Lady's Sensibilities Allowed at
THE LUCKY STRIKE HOUSE

'I don't understand this at all, Mr Paxton,' said Tom. 'This Granger fellow represented himself to be an old friend of my father's. We thought he was a respectable gentleman, but this. . . .'

'I'll tell you the way of it,' said Mr Paxton gently. 'We apprehend that this man asked round about the names and circumstances of families living out of town. He then turned up where there were young girls with a lot of cock-and-bull stories and lured a number of girls off by buying them clothes and such. I'm sorry to hear that Kathleen was one of them. If it's any consolation to you, I can say that if he appears in this area again it will be more than tarring and feathering that he'll get.'

'But what am I to do?'

'I don't know, son, I'm sure.'

'Can I have this handbill,' asked Tom Hogan, 'To show my ma, like?'

'Yes, yes, you take it away.'

All the way home Tom kept turning over in his mind what was to be done and the only thing he could come up with was that he would have to go to this Diamond City and bring Kathleen home.

It took some time to bring his mother to an appreciation of the danger into which her beloved daughter had fallen, but when once she understood the peril Melanie Hogan was most agreeable to Tom's going across the state to find his sister and bring her home. There was no cash money to be found for railroads or stages, so he would have to walk, and hitch rides on wagons and carts when he was able.

'If you can let me have some food, Ma,' said the boy, 'then that will keep me going for a time. I will take my rifle with me. I mind that there may be hazards on the road of which I know naught. Still and all, the thing must be done. It is not to be thought of to leave Kathleen in such places. And I shall speak a word or two to that Granger fellow if once I catch up with him.'

It might be mentioned in passing that Tom Hogan was a crack shot with his pa's rifle and could bring down pretty well anything that crawled or ran on the earth or flew in the sky.

The next day at dawn Tom set off along the road east, which headed towards Confederate Gulch and Diamond City. He knew nothing of these locations, save that gold had been found there in recent years and word was that they now rivalled the California goldfields of 1849. He had his rifle slung over his shoulder, a canteen of water, flask of powder and a bag of vittles, put together by his mother.

It was a fine enough day in late spring and, had it not been for the serious nature of his journey, Tom Hogan might have been smiling with the pleasure of being freed from the back-breaking toil of the farm. Lord knew how his ma would manage without either of her strong children, but there it was. He was lucky enough to be able to beg lifts from a succession of farm wagons and so on, making good time on the whole.

The day was nearly done and he was thinking about finding a haystack in which to spend the night, when trouble came looking for Tom. In those first few years after the end of the War between the States, there were any number of shiftless men who took up as road agents or what is known in England as 'highwaymen'. They robbed lone travellers of their money and anything else that might be worth stealing. Tom knew nothing of such things and did not know what the play was when two young men about ten years older than him, rode up, while he was trudging along the road on foot, and demanded that he hand over his money.

'Money?' said Tom in surprise, 'I ain't got a cent to my name. Anyways, even had I money, I don't see that I would be giving it to you.'

'No?' said one of the men. 'You have a big mouth

on you, boy.'

Tom Hogan did not care for the way that this conversation was proceeding and he had begun to unsling his rifle from his back, when both men drew and cocked their pistols.

'You make any move and you are as good as dead,' the man who first had spoken to him said with great assurance. 'Just you let fall that rifle on the road there. Touch the trigger or even look as though you will and it is all up with you.'

Very slowly, because he had the notion that these were men who meant what they said, Tom let the rifle slip to the ground.

'Now you step right away from it, you hear what I tell you?' said the other of the two men, who had not yet spoken. Tom moved back a few paces and the man dismounted. Then everything happened right fast. Tom dived for the rifle, which was, by the by, loaded, intending to get the drop on the two men. As he reached down for it the man who had got off his horse swung his pistol into the side of Tom's head. The blow made him feel sick and giddy, but he was a game one and kept scrabbling for his rifle. The man pistol-whipped him into submission and when he came to, Tom was lying in the road, bloodied and without a possession in the world. So vexed had the men been at his unexpected resistance that they had even taken his bag of food, canteen of water and flask of powder. It was nearly dusk and here he was with not a thing in the world, other than the very clothes upon his back.

There were boys of that age who would have despaired and given up altogether at this point, but Tom Hogan was not one of them. He picked himself up from the road, dusted his self down, checked that his injuries amounted to no more than a sore head and a few cuts, and then set off in the same direction as he had been travelling when the road agents waylaid him. He was a game one all right.

It was almost entirely dark, when Tom saw the lighted window of a log cabin ahead of him. He wondered if the occupant of such a lonely habitation would take kindly to a vagabond knocking at the door and begging a crust of bread and a swig of water. There was only one way to find out, so he trudged along until he reached the little hut, for it was in truth nothing more, and then rapped smartly upon the door.

A voice from within cried, 'Who's there? Stand to now, unless you want a minie ball through you!'

'Don't shoot, sir,' said Tom. 'I mean no harm. I have been set upon and robbed and wanted only a morsel of bread. It doesn't matter, I will not trouble you further.' He began to walk away from the log cabin, when the door opened and a man came out with a storm lantern in one hand and a rifle in the other.

'Hold up,' said the man. 'Don't be too hasty. I have to be a little rough on strangers, living out here. There are many types as would take advantage of an old man like me. Come in, come in and set down.'

Tom turned back and entered the cabin. It was a

perfectly decent little place, snug as could be, if only consisting of one large room. The owner looked to be a tad above sixty years of age and his hair was snowy white. It was his face that attracted the attention at once, because a great, jagged scar ran down one side of it. He wore an eyepatch on that same side, so presumably whatever misfortune had scarred him so had also cost him the sight of his eye. He saw that Tom was staring and he laughed.

'A bear did this, boy. Better part of forty years ago. I settled him though. He marked me for the rest of my life, but his own life was short enough. I killed him not five minutes after he did this to my face.'

Tom Hogan hardly knew what to say to such an assertion and limited himself to remarking that the bear must have been a big one.

'You got that right.' said the old man. 'Mind, it looks to me like you been in the wars somewhat on your own account.'

'This?' said Tom, touching his head and finding to his surprise that his fingers came away covered with blood. 'It is nothing to speak of. Some men stole my rifle. I tried to stop them and this is what resulted.'

'Stole your rifle, hey?' said the man. 'You are powerful young to be roaming the land with a rifle. You are not on the scout, up to some outlaw game, I hope?'

'No, nothing of the sort,' said the boy, a little shocked that he might be suspected of such an occupation. 'It is a long story.'

'I'll be bound,' said the old man. 'Well, here's the

15

way of it. My name is Caleb Walker and this here is my home, such as it is. I am about to eat and you are surely welcome to share my vittles if you are hungry. This is only my Christian duty towards any traveller. Then, if you are minded, you can tell me your story as payment for the meal. Does that strike you as a good bargain?'

After they had eaten fried squirrel and plantain, the old man took out a pipe, lit it up and invited Tom to tell him how matters stood. When he had heard the story, Walker said nothing for a bit, then remarked, 'And so you are aiming to bring back your sister from this den of iniquity, is that the strength of it?'

'Yes sir,' said Tom. 'That is my intention.'

'Some of them saloons, what they call hurdy gurdy houses and such, are powerful wicked places, son. You might find that they do not take kindly to giving up one of the girls who they have set up there. Have you thought on this?'

'I have. That is why I brought my rifle along. But now. . . .'

'Can you shoot?' asked the old man.

'With a rifle? Yes sir, I get by.'

Caleb Walker stood up suddenly and said, 'Show me.'

He picked up his rifle and led the way outside. It was almost dark, but the moon had risen. 'See that silver birch over yonder? The sapling, there.' He pointed to a slender tree, no more than two inches wide, which was growing some twenty-five yards from the back of the cabin.

'I see it,' said Tom Hogan. 'Then what?'

'Reckon you could hit it with this here rifle?' asked Walker.

'That I could,' said the boy with perfect assurance. Caleb Walker handed him the rifle and without taking pause, Tom cocked the piece, raised it to his shoulder and fired, all in one smooth, unbroken motion. The tree splintered at about four feet from the ground.

'God almighty,' said Walker in amazement. 'You surely can shoot. That is about the height from the ground of a man's heart as well. Tell me, was that by chance or design?'

'I did it apurpose, sir,' said Tom.

'Well, boy,' said the old man, 'if you have told me no lies and the case is as you have represented it to be, it might be that I can offer you some help. I have no love for the sort of men who lure innocent girls to their destruction in this wise and if I can frustrate their plans, then I am glad to do so. You can stay here tonight, and in the morning we will talk more on this.'

CHAPTER 2

The next day Caleb asked Tom, 'Well boy, are you still minded to go ahead with this enterprise of yours?'

'I don't see that I have another choice, sir,' replied the boy.

'I suppose that I had best give you some help then. You shoot well enough with a rifle, but what of pistols? You ever fire one?'

'I have done in the past. I am not as handy with them as I am with a rifle though.'

'Let's see if we can remedy that.'

The old man opened up a trunk, which he dragged from under his bed. He unlocked it and then took out a tooled leather gunbelt. Then he withdrew a cloth-wrapped bundle. This turned out to contain a pistol.

'Ever use one of these before?' he asked Tom.

The boy took it in his hands and spun the cylinder. 'I fired the Army model a few times at a neighbour's place. This is a Navy Colt, ain't it?'

'Yes, that's right. Want to give it a try?'

Caleb charged the chambers with powder and lead and fitted copper percussion caps over the nipples. Then they went outside together.

'Here now,' he said, handing the pistol to Tom. 'See if you can serve that birch in the way that you did with my rifle yesterday.'

The boy took hold of the revolver and aimed it carefully at the tree. He hesitated for a moment, and then fired. The shot went wide. He tried again and the same thing happened. He said, 'I am better suited to a rifle, I think.'

'That's a lot of nonsense. A good shot is a good shot, whether he's using a rifle or pistol. You know what the problem is? You're thinking about it too much. Last night you just brought up that rifle and fired, without giving it a second thought. We need you to use the same dodge with this pistol. Wait here.'

Walker went back into his cabin and then emerged with the black gunbelt. 'Here,' he said, 'Try this.'

Tom Hogan buckled on the holster and belt and placed the pistol in the holster. Then he drew, cocked and fired, without splitting the actions up at all, just as he always did with his rifle. The ball struck the tree this time, keyholing yesterday's bullet hole.

'There,' said Caleb Walker. 'You have the measure of it now. I'll warrant that before the morning's over, you'll be a regular crack shot with that thing, not a whit worse than you are with a rifle.'

So it proved, because before they broke off to eat

19

at midday Tom was drilling anything he set his mind to. Just as the old man had said, if you were a good shot with a rifle, then you could handle a pistol all right as well.

After they had eaten Caleb said to the boy, 'Well son, I don't gauge that I can teach you anything in the shooting line, other than how to load this thing. We shall spend an hour on that and then that is all you will need.'

'But I don't have a gun of my own,' said Tom, a little puzzled as to where this could all be tending.

'Why, you young fool, don't you grasp that I am about to let you borrow my own pistol?' said Walker, and he laughed.

'That's real kind of you, sir, but I can't make off with your gun like that.'

'Why boy, you don't think that this is the only one I possess? Not likely. Sit you down and I will tell you the way of it.' When they were both sitting at their ease on the turf, Caleb Walker continued: 'I was what they used to call a gunfighter at one time. I stopped all that foolishness years ago, once I reached a certain time of life, but that does not mean that there is no use in this world any more for guns and shooting. That story about your sister made me good and mad. If I was a younger man, I would come right with you to Diamond City and settle those villains for you, just for the sake of seeing them in hell. There is no low, slinking thing that crawls on the face of the earth that is worse than them as preys on innocent women and girls. I hates them more than I can say.'

'It's very good of you to help me like this, sir,' ventured Tom.

'Good? Nothing! It's like I say, I wish I had the strength that once I possessed to help you with this task. But I am doing what I am able, which is to fit you out for the job. Make no mistake boy, that sister of yours has fallen in with a bad crew. Mind, there's a good side to the case as well.'

'There is?' exclaimed the boy. 'I would be mighty obliged were you to point it out to me, because I cannot see the good part of this business myself.'

'It is like this. Would you say that your sister is a good girl?'

'You mean virtuous and such? Yes, she is.'

'Well then, there is this. Most of those pretty waiters, as they are called, are not forced into going with men, not if they don't want to. As long as they dance with them and make sure that the men spend their money in the hurdy house, that is all good enough for the owners of them places. If your sister has resisted the temptation to take the wrong path, why, you will fetch her back home with no damage to her at all.'

'I don't know,' said Tom. 'How I can ever repay you for this, sir?'

Walker said, 'The only repayment I require from you, young man, is to see you and your sister return along this road in a short while and for you to give me a true and particular account of your adventures. That will be plenty and enough payment. I would not mind that gun back as well, if you could manage it.'

Later that same afternoon Tom Hogan set off on his way again, only this time with a gun at his hip and a fixed determination that nobody had better trouble him again before he reached Confederate Gulch. Old Mr Walker had given him powder and lead, as well as a bag of food and an old canteen to replace those that had been stolen from him. His heart was feeling a good deal lighter as well, partly through finding such a good man who had been willing to help him out in this way.

The other thing that made him feel better was what the old man had said regarding the life lived by such girls as his sister had now become. He had had a suspicion that she would have been forced into all manner of beastliness and he would rather have seen her dead than succumb to such a degradation. If what Caleb Walker said was true, then her virtue would be sufficient to guard her against such a horror. Nevertheless, he had best not lose any time in bringing her home again.

It took Tom Hogan three days to reach the neighbourhood of Confederate Gulch; the largest settlement of this area was Diamond City. From all that he was able to collect from talking to people along the way, calling Diamond City a city was stretching the truth somewhat. There had, it seemed, been not a single building on the spot until three years previously.

The area was known as Confederate Gulch on account of it was there that two escaped Confederate prisoners had struck gold in 1864, not long before the end of the war. They had found a rich and prosperous seam of gold and a shanty town had sprung up as others flocked to the spot. It was this onetime shanty town that now went by the name of Diamond City and was home to some thousands of prospectors and others. The prospectors got rich by finding gold and many other people grew rich by cheating them of their wealth in various ways.

As far as Tom could make out, most of those in Diamond City made a living from supplying the prospectors with food, drink, clothes, tools and women. It made his blood boil to think that his own sister was now classed in this way; as a commodity to be bought and sold to miners and prospectors. Once he had rescued her from that place there would be a reckoning with those who had conspired to put her in such a false position.

Tom consulted the business card that Granger had left his mother on his departure. It gave a respectable sounding address, with no mention of the Lucky Strike, the saloon that featured on the handbill that he had been distributing around Cooper's Creek. It seemed to the young man that finding Granger and speaking to him man to man might be the best way of beginning this quest.

Diamond City was at that time the largest town in the whole of Montana. Everybody, it seemed, wished to share in the good fortune of the gold prospectors. There was so much gold floating around that all one needed to do was set up a little shop in Diamond City and one's fortune was made. The men who struck gold were not in general tight-fisted with their wealth, but often spent money as fast as they made it. It was not uncommon for a man to find a hundred dollars' worth of gold one day and have disposed of it before going to sleep that same night. Many of the saloons, brothels and gambling-houses took payment only in gold. A pinch of gold dust would buy a shot of whiskey and a nugget half the size of a pea would buy a woman for the night.

It did not take Tom Hogan long to discover that the address on Granger's visiting card did not exist. Although this did not come as too much of a surprise, there was still something a little shocking about a man having a bunch of cards printed with false details upon them.

Everything in the town looked so expensive and Tom did not have one cent to his name. Still and all, he was a resourceful lad and it did not take him long to figure out how to make some money.

Most of Diamond City's buildings were built of wood, but on the very outskirts of the town were tents where some of the men who catered for the lower end of the market had set up shop. A number of these were gambling dens, and Tom stood in the crowd and watched the play, so as to get the hang of the different games on offer. The one upon which he finally settled was called faro.

Faro is an easy enough game to play, even for a beginner. A set of cards from ace to king is painted on a large board or cloth laid over a table. Only the values of the cards matter and it does not signify what suit they are. Those wishing to play do so by putting their stake upon one of the cards. A pack of cards is placed in a wooden box called the shoe and cards are then drawn two at a time by the dealer. The first card drawn is the 'banker's card' and if you have bet on that number you lose your money. The second card is the 'player's card' and any stakes on that are returned, doubled, to the player. In other words, if you bet on the eight and the banker's card is an eight, you lose. If you have bet a dollar on the four and that is what the player's card is, you get two dollars.

Now the thing about faro is that you can calculate the odds and this gives you an edge over the banker; at least it can if you pay strict heed to which cards have been played and bet accordingly. There would be no point betting on the king if all four kings had already been drawn from the shoe, to give a simple example.

After standing and watching the play at the faro table for a time Tom worked out a most cunning and audacious ruse. It was not strictly honest, but then he felt that when his beloved sister's honour was at stake, any stratagem was justified. Some of the gamblers were playing with silver dollars and so on, but most were casting little buckskin bags on the table and announcing the weight of gold contained in them. So fast was the play that it was impossible for the banker to check the contents of each and every bag and a certain amount of honour was taken for granted.

It was not only honour that kept cheats in check. Anybody caught trying to defraud other players would face summary justice on the spot. It was not unknown for men to be beaten to death when detected in the act of cheating at cards. This being so, Tom's scheme was not without risk.

He left the tent and went down the way a little. When he had found a private spot he cut a small piece from the buckskin shirt that he was wearing and fashioned from it a little bag, of the sort commonly seen on the tables. This he filled with fifteen of the lead balls which Caleb Walker had given him as ammunition for the pistol. Then, his heart pounding painfully in his chest, he returned to the faro table.

It might be mentioned here that Tom Hogan, although he had received little enough schooling, had two skills. One, as we have seen, was a certain facility in the use of firearms. For a boy growing up in that time and place, this was perhaps nothing to remark upon. The other was certainly uncommon, though, for an unlettered farm boy. Tom had an uncanny ability to figure and cipher, particularly when it came to remembering sequences of numbers. He was able, and had demonstrated this as a trick to his mother and sister, to memorize a pack of cards and then recite them backwards and forwards after studying the pack for a minute or two. He had little thought that this knack would ever come in useful in his life.

Tom watched through an entire game, in order to

be sure that he understood what was required. Then, two-thirds of the way through the next game, he cast his little bag carelessly on the nine, saying, 'Six ounces there.' Nobody took any especial notice and the next player's card was indeed the nine of hearts. He casually accepted the little bag of gold which was given to him in addition to his own stake of lead bullets. So far, so good.

By carefully studying the play and not betting unless he was almost certain what he was about, Tom Hogan converted the fifteen bullets into no less than eighteen ounces of gold, worth, at the price then current, a little shy of $500. It was more money than he could ever have conceived that he would possess in his life, and he left the faro table feeling a little light-headed at the ease with which he had accomplished this trick.

As he left the tent, one of those watching said to him, 'Hell boy, you surely bucked the tiger there!'

'I don't take your meaning.' said Tom.

'Meaning that you won and that the bank is down on the deal,' said the man, with an amused glint in his eyes. 'Country boy, are you?'

'That don't signify,' said Tom, a little stiffly. 'Why do you ask?'

'No reason,' said the stranger. 'Don't take on so.'

This was the first person with whom Tom had exchanged more than the odd word since arriving in Diamond City and he thought it might be profitable to ask a few questions. 'Tell me now,' he said, 'Do you know a place called the Lucky Strike?'

'I should just about say that I do. And if you take my advice, son, you will give it a wide berth. They would eat you alive there.'

'What do you mean? I heard that it was somewhere that you could dance and drink. Is that not the case?'

'You surely are fresh and green, straight in from the country!' exclaimed the man, who was perhaps forty or thereabouts, 'Come, take a turn with me down the street aways.'

With a certain reluctance Tom walked with the man towards the centre of town. As they walked the fellow said, 'Listen, the Lucky Strike is set up to relieve men of their money. You have to pay to dance with the girls there and the drinks are real pricy. Not to mention where a lot of the girls are in business.'

'In business?' asked Tom, dreading the answer and hoping that he had misunderstood.

'Yes, yes,' said the man impatiently, 'in business. They are whores. Not all of them, mind, but enough to make it an unsavoury kind of place for a young fellow such as yourself.'

The two of them parted amicably and Tom went to find somewhere to stay for the night. He suddenly felt awful young and inexperienced and was sure that everybody he met would know it. Had he but realized it, this was not at all the appearance that he presented. True, he was young, but he was also heeled: carrying a gun. He had the air about him of a young man who was confident that he knew how to use a gun as well, which was not always the case with those who carried iron in that town.

Not everybody was able to read these signs, though, and while he was walking the streets, trying to choose a hotel which looked respectable, a drunk chanced to stagger against him. Tom was almost knocked into the road and said, mildly enough, 'Hey, careful there!'

'You say what, you whore's son?' said the man who had bumped into him, whirling round angrily.

'You came near to knocking me over,' explained Tom, not at all quarrelsome, but in the most reasonable way imaginable.

'Knock you over? I'll do more than that if you don't shut up and be on your way.'

'You have no occasion to speak to me so,' said Tom Hogan slowly. 'It is ill-mannered and uncalled for.'

One of the drunken man's companions (he was in a group of three or four) said, 'Don't provoke him, son. You just get on your way and leave us be.'

'I am not out to provoke anybody,' said Tom. 'If nobody troubles me, then I'm sure I don't look for to start an argument.' He turned and began to walk off, thinking that some of the people here seemed pleasant enough, but that others were plainly spoiling for a fight.

'Hold it right there, you cow's son,' said the man who had stumbled into him. 'Unless you're yellow, you will turn right round and face me like a man.'

'I ain't yellow,' said Tom, turning quickly to face the fellow. 'What did you have in mind?' One thing Tom knew for sure was that he did not aim to allow anybody to serve him as those two road agents had a few days ago. If this fellow wanted trouble, well then he, Tom Hogan, was ready to oblige him.

'Seth, no,' said one of the other men, 'He's only a kid. Leave him be.'

'I'll leave him be, maybe, if he tells me sorry for weaving all over the sidewalk and banging into me like that.'

'There you are, son,' said one of the group. 'You can see he's in liquor. Only say "sorry" and we can all go about our business, peacable like.'

Tom thought the matter over and saw the sense in it. He had more important fish to fry than this drunken fool. Then he remembered being pistol-whipped by the two road agents and said, 'No. If any apologizing is done, it had best be your partner here. It was him as banged into me.'

The man who had accosted him looked sobered on hearing this. He said, 'You boys stand aside now. I will settle this runt, once for all.' There were protestations from his friends, who, in all fairness, were trying to prevent what they saw as a helpless young boy from being needlessly killed. It was true that Tom was wearing a gun, which made a challenge like this quite legitimate; but none of them dreamed that he would actually be able to acquit himself well in any contest of this sort.

'Stand back, I say,' said the drunk once more. 'Well boy, are you going to say "sorry" or will you give me satisfaction?'

'I do not want to fight,' said Tom, 'but if you draw on me, before God, I will kill you.'

This was all it needed to set the tragedy in motion, because no sooner had Tom Hogan spoken those words than the drunk went for his pistol. His hand had closed over the hilt and it was halfway out of the holster when Tom's bullet took him in the chest, sending him sprawling in the road.

The man's companions gazed in horror at the dying man who lay bleeeding in the dirt of the roadway. They turned to Tom, who still had the Navy Colt in his hand.

'You men bear witness that I did not start that,' Tom said. There was a shocked silence, during which the boy replaced his pistol in the holster and continued along the same way that he had been going before the incident with the drunk had taken place.

CHAPTER 3

As he walked away from the scene of the confrontation, Tom half-expected for a sheriff or marshal to haul him back and throw him into jail. Nothing of the sort happened, though, and the dead man's friends did not seem disposed to make anything further of the matter, so he was evidently free to go. Truth to tell, shootings of that kind were far from being an uncommon occurrence in Confederate Gulch at that time. What with rows about claim-jumping, arguments about women, accusations of cheating at cards and practically every man in the district liquored up half the time and mostly carrying guns, the miracle of it was that there were not more killings.

It was not until he was some way down the street that the thing became real to Tom Hogan. He had done murder and for the most trifling of causes. Farm boys like Tom, though, were used to killing animals and birds as a matter of routine and were not so delicate about shedding blood as perhaps a youth living in the city might be. It was still a shock to him that he had shot a man, but he was a phlegmatic and unimaginative young man, and after being jumped by the robbers he had sworn to himself that he would not allow of any such liberties from any man in the future. Since nobody else seemed to be treating the matter as being particularly serious, he didn't see why he should do so himself.

By the time that Tom had found a nice looking hotel in which to stay he had more or less put the whole thing out of his mind. That is to say, he had stuffed it into that compartment of his mind where he was wont to hide all those various peccadillos which he was unwilling to face up to at the present time. He would reason the case out one day, when he had the leisure to do so.

He did not realize it, but this was exactly the type of mental gymnastics engaged in by many of the more ruthless gunfighters. They simply didn't think too long or hard about their killings. It was unfortunate that such an essentially decent young man as Tom Hogan should have been put in a spot where he was compelled to resort to such self-deceit at such a tender age.

After booking into a hotel that looked better than most, Tom had a bite to eat and then headed over to the Lucky Strike to look for his sister. He had no very clear idea of what he would do when he found her. Indeed, he did not even know if it was at the Lucky Strike that she was working. Granger had not talked of the place when he visited their farm; it was only from the handbill that Mr Paxton had given him that he had got the name of the place. Tom was still hoping against hope that there was a genuine mistake and that maybe his beloved sister Kathleen was really working at a proper theatre somewhere.

The Lucky Strike was not a particularly grand saloon. There were others in Diamond City that had plusher seats, bigger mirrors and more elaborate chandeliers, but the chief attraction of the Lucky Strike lay not in its interior decorations, but rather in the services that it offered. In most saloons in mining towns like this there were no women to be found at all, other than the occasional prostitute. In some of them, matters were so desperate that the men took to dancing with each other. This was not necessary at the Lucky Strike.

Saloons like the Lucky Strike were known as hurdy-gurdy houses because, at one time, the girls in them really did play hurdy gurdys to entertain the customers. These days though, they were more often called 'Pretty waiter houses'. The aim was to separate men from their money as expeditiously as possible. The customers had to pay to dance with the girls and were also expected to buy them drinks. These drinks, despite the exotic names on the bottles, were really no more than coloured sugar-water. The management did not want any of the girls becoming intoxicated, because then they were incapable of generating income by flirting and dancing with the men who frequented the house. It only took one such girl to create havoc on the dance floor. It was said that: 'A hurdy gal on a drunk raises more hell than a locoweed-fed bull', and it was quite true.

The fellow at the door of the Lucky Strike looked Tom over carefully and decided that he was old enough to enter and probably flush enough to waste his substance in their house to their advantage. He was nodded through. As soon as he was through the door, a young girl dressed, to Tom's mind, in an indecently short skirt came up to him and asked if he would dance with her.

'I am not much of a one for dancing, miss,' he told her politely, 'but I am obliged to you for the offer.'

'Oh please,' said the girl, who could have been no older than Kathleen, 'The boss gets riled up if we don't dance at least ten dances every evening. It's only a dollar.'

'All right then,' said Tom, thinking that this might be as good a way as any to seek news of his sister. 'I will dance the next dance with you, miss.'

'Lord,' The girl giggled. 'Ain't we grand? There's no miss in the case, my name is just Jane. We don't run much to fancy manners here.'

'Well then, Jane,' he said, 'you fetch me when the next dance is going to begin. I shall be over yonder at the bar.'

It felt very grown-up to be drinking in a saloon. Tom knew that if ever his ma learned that he had been in such, she would never recover from the shock. Still, now he was here, he figured he might as well make the most of the experience. He ordered a beer, which request was contemptuously brushed aside.

'We don't serve beer here, son,' the barkeep told him, 'Nor soda pop, mineral water or milk neither. There's whiskey, absinthe and a variety of fancy foreign liqueurs, but nothing in the beer line.'

'Then it will be whiskey, please,' said Tom. He had only tried spirits once and they had not altogether agreed with his constitution. He paid for the drink with a pinch of gold dust and surveyed the dance floor. He couldn't see Kathleen anywhere and resolved to ask Jane about her when they were dancing. The music was provided by three men up on a stage set at one end of the room. One played a violin, one a piano and the third beat out a rhythm on a little drum. Even to a youngster like Tom, with little experience of the world, the Lucky Strike seemed a wretched sort of a spot to spend one's time. None of the girls looked all that happy and neither did the men. He couldn't see the attraction of it.

Jane came and fetched him when the next dance started. He paid her the equivalent of a dollar and signed her card for her. The whole thing was about as romantic as buying a can of lamp oil at the general store.

'Have you worked here for long?' he asked Jane as they took to the floor.

'Why are you asking me that?' the girl said suspiciously. 'You are not working for the marshal's office or aught of that sort?'

Tom laughed. 'Do I look old enough to be a deputy?'

'I guess not, but you can't be too careful. I have been here almost a year.'

'Do you know a girl called Kathleen?'

'No, I don't, and you are getting me worried. Have you come here to dance and drink or only to ask a lot of foolish questions?'

'I am trying to find my sister. A fellow called Granger offered her work and he said that he came from this town. There, I have been honest with you. There is nothing to do with marshals or sheriffs. I am hoping to find my sister and take her home with me.'

'That's the way of it, is it? I might be able to help, but it will cost you a deal more than the dollar you paid for this dance.'

'I will pay what is needful. Do not try to trick me though. Because it won't answer.'

'You are mighty strong-willed for such a young boy. I bet you are no older than me.'

'It is no secret. I am seventeen, the same age as my sister.'

The musicians brought the piece to a close and Jane said, 'Book me for the dance after next and we will talk some more. You have to buy me a drink now. It's what is done.'

Tom bought her a poisonous-looking, bright-green liquid which was in a bottle with an ornate label written in some foreign language. The girl went off to the side, ready to dance with the next poor fool who had engaged to give her a dollar for the privilege. At

37

least she was willing to talk to Tom about his sister. Of course, she might be planning to cheat him out of his money, but he didn't think so. His guess was that she really knew something about Kathleen.

The whiskey had tasted every bit as foul as he recalled from the last time that he had tried some. Nobody seemed bothered that he was not drinking much himself. As long as he was dancing and buying the girl drinks, that was all that was expected.

After the next dance ended, Jane came over to him and said, 'Well, you're next.'

Once they were on the floor again, Tom said, 'What can you tell me about my sister?'

'It's more than my life is worth to talk about this here,' said Jane. 'After we close up you will have to pretend that you have made a deal with me.'

'What sort of deal?' asked Tom, mightily perplexed.

'To screw me, of course,' said the girl in surprise, 'What sort of deal did you think I meant? To buy a wagon and horses or something?'

'I am not up to all this sort of life, miss.'

'I told you, don't call me miss. It makes me sound like somebody's maiden aunt.'

'What time do you leave here?'

'That depends. Why don't you meet me outside at about two.'

'Two in the morning?' asked Tom, aghast. 'Lord, I should hope to be in my bed at that hour.'

'Well, it's up to you. If you want to know what's what, then you will meet me here at two. Otherwise, don't you bother. It is a risk for me that I am none too keen to take. I only offered to help because I like the look of you.'

'I thought you said you would want to be paid for any information you give me?' Tom reminded her.

'Yes, well I am not one of these rich philanthropists that you hear tell of. I have to eat and drink and pay for my lodgings,'

After the dance had finished Tom Hogan said to the girl, 'Well, I guess that I will meet you outside at two, if that is agreeable.'

'Yes, and don't be late.'

After leaving the Lucky Strike the young man wandered the streets for a while, trying to figure out whether he was doing the right thing. He was sure that the girl who was offering to sell information about his sister was a mercenary wretch, but she was the only trail that he had to follow. That being so, he saw little choice but to meet her and pay whatever she demanded for news of Kathleen's whereabouts.

Diamond City was a lively, bustling town and unlike Cooper's Creek, which tended to quieten down as the evening drew on, Diamond City seemed to grow more boisterous with every hour that passed. Tom had nothing with which to compare it, but it struck him that if all large towns were anything at all like this, then he was glad that he lived out in the wilds. He had never seen so many people in the whole course of his life as he saw on this one evening here.

At a quarter before two Tom Hogan was waiting

outside the Lucky Strike for Jane to appear. She didn't leave until it had passed the half hour, although he had no way to gauge the time. All he knew was that he felt mighty tired. Jane looked as perky as she had five hours earlier, although she must have been dancing almost continuously since last he saw her.

She greeted him with a smile, saying, 'I wondered if you'd show up or not.'

'I said I'd be here, didn't I?'

'Folk don't always do what they say they will,' said the girl. 'Let's take a walk.'

Jane led him through the streets, which had at last calmed down a little. She did not speak until they were on the very edge of town and she could be sure that nobody could overhear what she was saying. Then she said,

'I'm not going to take advantage of you. You seem like a nice boy and it would not be kind of me to do it. Come and sit with me on that wall over there and I will tell you the way of it. Then, if you think that what I have told you is worth hearing, you can pay me what you feel is right.'

This was fair-spoken and Tom felt ashamed of doubting the girl's sincerity. They went over to a low wall and sat down side by side.

Jane said, 'I asked about your sister. I hear where she came and worked for a spell at another of the hurdy houses that Granger has an interest in. It is called the Girl of the Period and it is on the other side of town from where I work. My friend told me that she did not fit in at all and would not entertain men or nothing of that sort.'

'I should think not indeed,' said Tom. 'The very thought of it! What happened then?'

Jane said, 'Girls like me, we sometimes go with men and other times not. It depends on how we feel and if we want to. The manager at the hurdy sometimes introduces us to men and then takes a split of the profits, but a lot of us make private arrangements of our own and there is little enough that the boss can do about it.'

Tom was aghast to hear this and said, 'What would your mother say if she knew all this?'

'That's nothing to the purpose,' said Jane. 'I have not seen my mother for some good, long while. Anyways, don't interrupt. Some of the men running the Lucky Strike and a few other hurdys have an interest in one or two cathouses. You know what a cathouse is, I suppose?'

'Yes, I know. You mean brothels. I am not a child.'

'No, but you are real innocent in some ways. I saw it as soon as you walked in tonight.'

'Go on, please,' said Tom. 'I am afeared of what you are about to tell me, but go on.'

'The thing that they have in the cathouses is that the girls often dig up and leave when they have a mind to. You can't keep them locked up and all those stories you hear about girls being forced into such a life is mostly a heap of foolishness. Most of them work there because they can't do anything else. But they leave when they want and don't do as they are bid, which makes running brothels a tiresome business for the boss. Till now, that is.'

'Why, what do you mean, till now? What has changed?'

'I will tell you,' said Jane. 'Do you know what morphine is?'

'I do not recollect hearing the word before. What does it signify?'

'You know about opium?'

'I heard of it,' said Tom. 'It's what Chinamen smoke, ain't it? Some kind of drug.'

'Morphine's made out of opium. It is stronger and once you are used to it, you have to have it, or you go crazy. They used it in the war for men in pain and some of them got so they could not live without it. There are thousands and thousands of men who are that way. They will do anything at all to get the stuff, because without it they hurt and feel like to die.'

'How does this touch upon my sister? I do not see where this is tending.'

'It is this way. One of the bosses at the Lucky Strike hit upon the idea that if he could get some girls so they could not do without the morphine, then they would not leave him. They would be tied to him because only he could get them what they needed. Then it would be like they were prisoners, because they would know that if they ran off or did not do as he bid them, then they would not get any of this morphine. Do you take me so far?'

'I never heard of such wickedness in all my born days,' said Tom Hogan. 'I tell you plain, I would kill this man like a dog.'

'He has some houses, not in town, but out of the way from here, where he takes girls that he finds and promises jobs to. He chooses them special. Then he keeps them locked up there and gives them morphine regular, whether they will or no. After a time they cannot live without it and then they are his entirely and will do whatever he wants.'

'Landsakes, you don't mean that you think he has my sister locked up in such a place?'

'To speak plain, I don't know. From what you tell me, I think it could be so. Leastways, this girl called Kathleen vanished and that is what the other girls guess had become of her.'

Tom was so disturbed that he jumped up and began pacing to and fro. He said, 'Jane, can you tell me where these houses are that you think the girls might be in?'

'There are two. They are farmhouses, pretty much in the middle of nowhere, so that any cries for help are apt to go unheeded. I have wrote down rough directions. There, that is all I can do for you.'

Tom Hogan took out one of the little bags of gold that he had won at the faro table. He handed it to the girl, saying, 'This is six ounces of gold. Please think about buying a ticket away from here with it. This is no life for a decent girl such as you.'

'I do all right here. But thank you for your gold.' To his surprise, she leaned over and kissed Tom on the cheek. 'You are a real sweet boy.' Then she walked briskly away.

On the way back to the hotel he was staying at, Tom Hogan reasoned the matter out in his head. He knew nothing about drug addiction or anything of that sort, but he felt that things were not as bleak as he had feared. He knew his sister. He was certain-sure that she would not have fallen for any of the blandishments of men at any hurdy house and that this was what had put it into the mind of the bosses to try and force her into being a bad woman.

Back at the hotel, which luckily for Tom had a night watchman whose job it was to let in customers who had been carousing the night away until all hours, he went to his room and decided that unless he got a good night's sleep, he would be fit for nothing, come the morrow. Having come to this decision, he undressed, climbed into bed and slept the sleep of the just until about eleven of the clock in the morning.

CHAPTER 4

Tom Hogan might only have been seventeen years of age, and wet behind the ears to boot, but he was very far from being a perfect fool. He knew that the enterprise which he was planning was a hazardous one and he intended to make good plans before he undertook anything. He might only be a simple farm boy, but he could see when he was about to take a big step.

Two things that he would be sure to need if he were to be successful in this current project were a horse and a good rifle. He had sufficient funds now to buy both without dickering over the price and so, after a substantial breakfast, he went off to try his luck.

Buying a rifle was the easiest thing in the world. Practically every man walking the streets of Diamond City was armed to the teeth and the trade in firearms was lively and brisk. Seeing that there was so much competition to sell guns, this had the effect of driving down the prices somewhat and Tom was able to buy a decent rifle for a sight less than he would have expected to do in Cooper's Creek. He had given ample proof the night before of his prowess with a pistol, but it was with rifles that he really felt at ease.

Renting a pony for a few days worked out a better deal for Tom than buying a horse outright. That would have entailed buying tack for the creature as well and this way, he could get all that thrown in with the hire price. Besides, once he had rescued Kathleen they could not both travel back home on the one horse. He chose a light skewbald pony which looked as though he had a bit of grit.

Before riding out it struck Tom that it might do no harm to have a look at the Girl of the Period saloon. He left the pony at the livery stable and set out across town on foot. Like as not, it would not even be open at this hour of the day, but there was no harm taking a peep at the place.

As he had half-suspected, the hurdy house was shut up and there was no sign of life. While he was looking at it from across the street, though, he saw a figure leave from a side exit. It was a Chinese boy of about the same age as him and, on impulse, Tom followed him.

When the boy cut down an alleyway Tom overtook him and said, 'I saw you come out of that saloon just now. Do you work there?'

The boy looked him over, as though working out whether he could lick Tom in a fight if there was need. Having evidently decided that he could, he said, 'Why you want to know? What business of yours?'

There was a vague recollection at the back of Tom's mind that he had heard somewhere that the Chinese were red hot on family and any loyalties that tended in that direction. He thought there was nothing to lose by turning his hand over and seeing what the other fellow would make of it.

He said to the Chinese boy, 'My sister was tricked into coming here by a bad man called Granger. She is a good girl, virtuous like, and thought that she would be acting on the stage. When she came here, she found that she was to flirt and dance with a lot of low men. Do you have a sister?'

There was a flicker of sympathetic interest in the other boy's eyes and he said, 'Yes. Two sisters. Good girls.'

'Why then,' said Tom, 'you must know just how I feel. Think if one of your own sisters was taken to such a house like that, how would you feel?'

'Bad place,' said the Chinese boy. 'Bad place, bad people.'

'What are you doing with them? Do you work there?'

'Not work. Run errands for my uncle. He sends things there.'

'Listen, I want to know if you can tell me anything that would help me find my sister. She was sent there and then left. I fear that she is being held a prisoner somewhere. If you can tell me anything that might help. . . .'

47

'All I can say is, take her home quickly. Some of those girls get like opium smokers. You know what is opium?'

'Yes, it's a drug.'

'Opium smokers no good for much. Boss at the saloon gives them much worse than opium. That's all.' The boy left without saying another word and Tom was left with the confirmation that Jane's story had not been a lot of moonshine. His mind was working fast, though, and he found it a curious coincidence that yesterday he had been talking about opium with Jane and then today a Chinese person showed up at one of the hurdy gurdy houses. Even out in Cooper's Creek, the association of opium and the Chinese was known. He wondered how big the trade in this morphine stuff was. Jane had talked of 'thousands and thousands' of men using it. Was this some big business like buying and selling liquor? And where did they get the opium? From the Chinese?

Despite his anxiety about Kathleen, Tom Hogan could not help but ponder such matters. After all, they touched upon the welfare of his sister and so needed to be considered anyway. He had a notion that he might find out more about all this at the houses that he was planning to visit that very day. He went back to the livery stable, collected the pony and set off.

The first farmhouse that he was aiming to visit was eight miles from Diamond City. According to the scrawled description that Jane had given him, it was pretty well fortified. How he would deal with this, he had no clear idea as of yet. The first thing was to get there and see the lie of the land.

The house stood off the road, at the end of a track about a half-mile long. From the road, it looked nothing remarkable; just a stone-built house with a collection of outbuildings scattered around it. A sort of native caution warned Tom that riding right up and rapping on the door might not be the smart dodge and so he carried on riding down the road and then, when once he was out of view from anybody who might be watching from the windows, he veered off and rode for a little copse of trees which grew on the crown of a rise of ground over-looking the house.

Once he reached the cluster of trees Tom dismounted and secured his pony to one of them. Then taking the new rifle in his hand, he moved forward until he had a good view of the house below. He lay down with the rifle in front of him and simply waited. He had done plenty and enough hunting not to find it irksome simply to lie quiet like this, watching and waiting. He could lie there all day if needs be. What he was waiting for, he could not say. Perhaps to see how many men were at the house or maybe to listen for screams or cries for help from his sister or any other poor girls who might be held captive there.

It was because his whole being was focused upon the house that Tom Hogan did not hear a stealthy figure creeping up behind him. The first he knew of the case was a sharp, metallic click right by his ear as a pistol was cocked. He craned his head round and met the coldest eyes he had ever seen in the whole course of his life.

Describing them later, he said that they were like holes leading nowhere: mineshafts or wells perhaps. Just empty and with nothing behind them.

'Don't you go moving a muscle, boy. Fact, don't you even speak, leastways not while I have this .45 right behind your ear.'

Given the circumstances, Tom felt no inclination either to move or speak.

The man continued, 'Now listen up, I'm agoing to reach down there and remove that pistol from your belt and then I'm going to take up that rifle. Still, don't you speak or move, you hear me? Just give a little nod if you are agreeable.' Tom nodded his head slightly.

When he had been relieved of his weapons, the man said, 'Nothing else I should know about, is there, boy? Derringers, knives, anything of the kind? You may speak now without fear.' Although he offered this assurance, Tom could not help but observe that the .45 was still aimed at his head. The man continued, 'Wriggle back a space, so that nobody in that there house can see us. You are setting fair to queer my pitch and that's a thing I will not endure.'

After Tom had wriggled back on his belly the man who had disarmed him went over to a tree and sat down, with his back leaning against it. He invited Tom to do the same, so that they could talk to each other.

'Are you working for the man who runs those hurdy houses?' asked Tom curiously.

'Nothing of the sort. Truth to tell, I was about to ask you the self-same question. Looking at you though, I see there is no need. You are only a boy. How old are you son?'

'I'm seventeen, sir.'

'You need not call me "sir". My name is Nathaniel Harker. You may call me Mr Harker or Nathaniel if you will. I answer to both. The point is, who are you and what are you doing here?'

'Are you the law?'

'Well now, that is what you might call a debatable point. I work for Pinkertons. You hear of us?'

'Detectives and such, ain't you?'

'Private detectives, yes. But the regular law use us sometimes to smoke out trouble. This is where the present case lies.'

'Why is the law interested in that house?' asked Tom. 'Is it on account of the girls?'

'What, you mean the hurdy girls? No, why should that be of interest? They all choose to be what they are. There is no crime in it. This is another matter entirely and I am glad to find that you know nothing of it.'

On impulse, Tom said, 'You mean about the morphine, then? I know about that too.'

'Do you, by God? You are playing a dangerous

game then. How much do you know?'

'If you are not the law, then I don't see that I need to be answering all the questions here. I don't reckon you have any more right to ask me questions than I have to ask them of you.'

Nathaniel Harker thought this over for a bit and then said, 'Well, but I have the drop on you. See where I have a .45 revolver pointing at you and you have no weapon at all.'

Tom's mind was working faster than he had ever known it to do, because spotted at once the flaw in the man's reasoning. He said to Harker, 'You want to do everything right secret. You wanted me to come away from the edge of this copse in case we were seen from the house. You fire that pistol and everybody down there will hear it. That will set the fox in the hen house or I miss my guess.'

'You are a right smart boy. That is how things stand. Suppose then that we sit here and reason together for a spell and see where it leads us?'

'All right,' said Tom. 'But I want my guns back. I mean you no harm and if you are against those villains down there, then I reckon we are on the same side, more or less.'

Harker considered this bold statement, then said, 'Go on then, take them back. You do not look as though you are the double-crossing breed.'

Tom sketched a brief outline of his mission to rescue Kathleen and fetch her back home, to which Harker listened with apparent sympathy.

While he was talking Tom examined the man hard

and could not quite make up his mind about the fellow. Nathaniel Harker, if indeed that was his real name, was aged about forty and as dark-complexioned as a Mexican or half-breed. His hair was that rich, lustrous black that has highlights of blue when the light falls upon it. There was no grey that Tom could see. He had a pleasant enough face, with a wide, mobile mouth which was as ready to smile as it was to frown. It was his eyes that were the dominant feature of the face. They were utterly cold and seldom blinked, putting Tom Hogan in mind of a rattlesnake. He had not the least doubt that this man was a killer, but then again, he remembered with a sudden shock, so too was he.

When Tom came to the part about the Chinese boy, Harker's ears pricked up and he said, 'Chinaman, hey? That's interesting and no mistake. You say he was going errands to the Girl of the Period? Yes, that all ties in.'

'Ties in with what, Mr Harker?' asked Tom. 'I have been open with you and you might now tell me what your business is here. You say that it is not girls, but you haven't said what you are doing up here, spying on that house. If it's not the girls, then what?'

'Don't crowd me, boy,' said Harker. 'I don't like it. For such a young fellow, you have a right pushy way about you that might put some folk's backs up. Give me breathing space and I will see what is fitting to tell you.'

'I did not mean to crowd you, sir. But if we have

finished here, then I am going down to yonder house to seek my sister.'

'Why, you damned young fool, it is not to be thought of! You will upset the apple-cart if you go blundering into this. Don't be an idiot.'

'Then tell me what your game is,' said Tom, 'And perhaps we can join forces.'

'Join forces with a mere child! You must be out of your mind. I have important business here.'

'Well then so do I. I don't see that my affair is any less urgent than yours.'

Nathaniel Harker looked at the young man before him with a mixture of irritation and amusement. He was strongly reminded of the way that he himself had been at that age: pig-headed, stubborn as a mule and determined not to let anybody push him around.

He said, 'Well, I suppose that you will be queering my pitch for me if I don't come to some accommodation with you. It's a damned nuisance. Can I not persuade you to ride on and leave this to me?'

'You already said that the hurdy girls are not important to you. One of them is all that matters to me, so I guess I will not leave the thing in your hands, no.'

'Very well then,' said Harker, 'here is how the case is situated. You have heard of morphine, which is like to opium, only far stronger. Do you know what a hypodermic is?'

'A hyper what?' asked Tom.

'A hypodermic needle is a hollow needle with a little glass tube at the back. You can deliver a drug right into your blood with it.'

'Sounds horrible.'

'It is that. During the late war, a lot of men who was injured got treated like that with morphine. It stopped the pain of their wounds, but it was so pleasant that they wanted to keep on using it, even after they had healed. There are, if you can believe it, nearly half a million such now.'

'Half a million,' cried Tom in surprise. 'Why, that cannot be true.'

'It's true enough,' said the Pinkertons man. 'There is only a small amount of this morphine being made officially, so some people have set up factories to make it and sell it to them as wants it. It is the biggest business you ever heard of, almost as big as the liquor industry. Thing is, son, those who use this stuff don't want to work or look after their families any more. All they want is to sit around taking morphine. They steal to pay for it and some girls end up in brothels so that they can keep getting it.'

'If you aren't after helping these girls, then why are you watching that place down there?'

'It's one of the factories where the stuff is made. They bring in opium and then cook it up into morphine. We are engaged in putting a stick in the spokes of their wheel, as you might put it.'

'I will help you now, if you help me to go after my sister. I can shoot.'

'I don't doubt you have shot a squirrel, but did you ever draw down on a living man and shoot him?'

'Yes, last night. I killed him, what's more.'

Harker stared at the young man and weighed the thing up. Then he made up his mind. 'All right then, it is a deal. I could do with an extra pair of hands. There are only three men down at that house and one of them is only a chemist. He will give us no trouble. Leave your horse up here.'

From what Harker had said there were no girls being held in this particular house; it was only being used to manufacture morphine. Harker's aim was only to destroy what there was of the substance here and then move to the next place.

Tom cocked his rifle and walked down the slope towards the back of the big old farmhouse. He noticed that there were stout wooden storm shutters on all the windows and, what was curious on a fine afternoon in late April, they were all fastened up. As Harker pointed out, this made it unlikely that anybody would spot them approaching. The Pinkertons man had become quite affable, when once he realized that Tom was not about to leave. It seemed to Tom that he liked somebody to talk to when he was up to these games and a young fellow like Tom was an ideal companion for him. There was no chance of a seventeen-year-old boy trying to take over the show and presumably Harker would not have to share the glory either if things went well. All in all, it seemed to Tom that Nathaniel Harker had got the best of the deal.

When the two of them were right at the back door of the farmhouse Harker indicated to Tom that they should go into the nearby barn and see what was going on there. There did not, to Tom's eyes, appear to be anything much of interest in the old barn; just large, wooden crates, packed with straw and each containing a dozen glass demijohns of a clear liquid. Harker uncorked one of the flagons and tasted the contents by the simple expedient of dipping in his finger.

'That's the stuff all right,' he said with great satisfaction. 'There must be close on a hundred gallons of it in this room. We have won the kitty here.'

'Is that it?' asked Tom. 'Is that all that you wished to see?'

'Not by a long chalk,' said the other. 'I mean to get inside that house and close down their damned factory entirely. If you want my help in freeing that sister of yours, then I heartily recommend that you help me in the endeavour.'

'What would you have me do?' asked Tom, with a distinct lack of enthusiasm.

'I think that you should just knock at that door, like you are a lone traveller or something of that sort. You look harmless enough, you are no more than a child. When the door is opened I will burst in and then, between us, we can clear the whole nest of them out.'

'Suppose they won't open the door for me?' objected Tom.

'Why then, you can make up some story to persuade them, I guess. Lord, what a one you are for raising foolish objections. Boys are not as adventurous as they were when I was your age. I would have given my eye teeth to be mixed up in a game like this when I was seventeen.'

With some trepidation Tom marched up to the door and knocked upon it. There was no response. Harker had crept up to one side and was now crouched by the door, out of sight of anybody within, or so Tom hoped. He felt very exposed, just standing here in the open.

He knocked again and this time a gruff-sounding voice asked what his business was. Tom had an inspiration and said, 'I have a meesage from a Chinese boy in Diamond City. He said I had to deliver it in person.'

There was silence for a minute or so, as though the man within was trying to work out if this was a true bill. He evidently decided that it was, because there was the sound of bolts being drawn and a rusty old lock turning. Then the door opened a crack and a fearsome-looking individual peered out and said,

'What is it?' The man's eye flicked down to the rifle that was in Tom's hand; he looked to be having second thoughts about the wisdom of opening the door. Tom could see what was going through his mind. The fellow was on the point of slamming the door shut when Nathaniel Harker lurched to his feet and slammed his not inconsiderable weight into the door, sending the man who had opened it flying backwards. As Harker moved, so too did Tom. In his case, his movement consisted of raising his rifle to cover the man who had answered his knock.

The Pinkertons man rushed into the kitchen and neatly disarmed the fellow who was now sprawled on the floor. He did this by clubbing the man round the head a couple of times until he fell back, stunned. Then Harker relieved him of his pistol and searched him.

There was dead silence in the rest of the house. Either there was nobody else in or the brief struggle in the kitchen had not been heard. Harker, his capable .45 at the ready, advanced into the passage that led to the rest of the house.

He had not taken three steps before he leaped back, shouting, 'Shit!' Somebody had taken a shot at him. He fired three shots from the doorway and into the passage, more or less at random.

Tom's heart was pounding so hard that he could scarcely breathe. This was not at all like the little incident the previous day, when he had shot the drunk. In that case, there had only been him shooting. Now, the bullets were flying towards him and he did not take to it at all. He and Harker waited and listened, but there was no further sound from the passage.

The Pinkertons man said softly to Tom, 'We will rush the hallway. Both of us together and firing as we go.' He said to the man who was now sitting on the floor of the kitchen, 'Let me see you try to take any action against us and I'll shoot you down like a dog. Is that clear?' The man nodded. He did not look as though he had much fight in him.

'Count of three!' said Harker. 'One, two, three!' The two of them charged along the passage, Harker firing a couple of shots and Tom holding fire until he had a target. They need not have troubled, though, because the man who had fired on Harker was lying dead at the foot of the stairs. Apparently one of the wild shots that Harker had sent in that direction from the kitchen, had found its mark.

'Well, that was lucky,' said Harker, looking down at the corpse.

'Not for him,' said Tom.

Harker shouted up the staircase, 'I know that there is another of you in this house. Anybody that don't want to get his self killed had best come forward now with his hands in the air. If I come up to search, then I am going to shoot anybody who has not surrendered.'

A quavery and high-pitched voice called back, 'Don't shoot, for God's sake. I'm coming down.' A thin, weedy-looking man in his middle years appeared at the top of the stairs, with his hands held up high above his head. 'What will you have?' he said, 'Do you want me to come down?'

Both Tom with his rifle and Nathaniel Harker with his pistol covered the man's descent. As he came down, the man said, 'I'm only a chemist, you know. I have no gun or any weapon at all.'

When he reached the bottom, Harker searched him scientifically and perhaps a mite more roughly than was strictly necessary. He was still perhaps feeling aggrieved at being shot at although, as a Pinkertons agent, he might reasonably have expected such things to occur from time to time.

Tom waited patiently, but was eager to get to the other house where his sister was probably being detained against her will.

Harker was in no particular hurry to leave, wanting to investigate the whole house with a thoroughness that Tom found maddening. They collected the other man from the kitchen, where he was still sitting in a dispirited fashion and, together with the little chemist, traipsed round every room, until Harker was satisfied that he had seen it all. The top floor had been converted into a laboratory, with glass tubing and retorts covering almost the whole of one wall. Here and there little spirit lamps powered whatever process was taking place. It put Tom Hogan in mind of a moonshine still that he had once visited at a neighbouring farm. The only difference was that in the still, the end product had been an evil smelling, dark liquid, whereas here it was white crystals.

'Tell me about these Chinamen who bring you the opium to work with,' suggested Harker amiably of the chemist.

'Oh, I don't see much of them,' began the little man, before the other man warned him to shut his mouth and say nothing. This did not go down well with the Pinkertons agent, who said,

'If you boys cooperate with me, I might try and put in a good word for you when you come to court.'

The chemist looked keen on the idea, but the other fellow simply laughed and said, 'What court? You ain't the law and you won't be getting us to no court. I know what you're about. You are being hired to disrupt our supply line. You will smash everything up here and then tell the marshals where to come.'

'Ain't you the bright one?' said Harker contemptuously. 'You don't know it all, so you best shut up yourself.'

In the end, things worked out just precisely as the man had predicted. Harker smashed up all the equipment and poured every drop of solution that he could find out on the earth. The white crystals he disposed of by casting them down the privy. The little chemist was horrified to see the fruits of his industry destroyed in this way.

'You are throwing away thousands of dollars there,' he told Harker. 'I am apt not to get paid for all this. I have a wife and children to feed, you know.'

'Is that a fact?' said Harker, with not a trace of sympathy in his voice. 'Maybe you'd better find a better line of work, then, rather than this filthy business. I have seen the harm caused by what you are making and I can tell you now that if I was in charge of the courts I would make it a hanging matter.'

'Yes,' said the man who had opened the door to them, 'but then you ain't in charge of any court. You have slowed up our operation here and wasted a lot of the good stuff, so having done your wrecking, maybe we can go now?'

There was little enough that Harker could have done, even had he wished, to bring the men to justice. He had no legal power of arrest and they were surely not going to cooperate by waiting there quietly while he went off and hunted for a sheriff. Besides, as had been intimated, his real purpose was to smash up the laboratory and destroy the morphine. He condescended to explain how matters stood to young Tom, after the other two men had departed.

'We are gradually getting on top of this racket. We break up factories such as this and make life hard for the men running them in a hundred different ways. It's working, too. There is a sight less morphine around now than there was last year, and in consequence the number of men dependent upon it is also falling. We will have it licked in a year or two.'

Although he was keen to be going Tom was interested, in spite of himself. 'Where does the opium come from?'

'It's smuggled over the border from Canada. It gets there from boats crossing the Pacific. It is landed at Vancouver, where there is the biggest Chinatown in North America. That's why I took heed when you told me about a Chinese boy visiting the Girl of the Period. It all fits together.'

'Can we be getting off now to that other house?' asked Tom. 'I am afeared that after all this ruckus, those men will go straight there as soon as they have left here. I do not want my sister to be moved somewhere else.'

'I never knew such an impatient young man as you,' said Harker disapprovingly. 'It is not becoming in one of such tender years. By the by, you stood up well under fire. I thought you might have cut and run.'

'I never cut and ran in my whole life,' said Tom.

CHAPTER 5

As Harker and Tom rode on towards the location of the other house about which Jane had given him information and which was seemingly known to the Pinkertons agent, the two of them fell into conversation. Tom asked Harker, 'How did you get into this work, sir?'

'When the war ended, I found that I was right good at killing folk and taking what I wanted. That's all well and good when there is a war on, but it is not what folk want to see when there is peace. I could have ended up getting myself hanged. My methods are a little too direct for regular law enforcement, so I found that Pinkertons was the best offer for me. I have been two years now with them.'

'You will help me to free my sister? Recollect that you gave me your word.'

'You are a prickly one! I have not forgot. It will be a harder row to hoe than that job we just undertook, though. As you say, those two scoundrels we freed will most likely go scooting straight off to raise the alarm.

It will be like laying siege to a fortress in time of war.'

'I'm game for that,' declared Tom curtly.

They rode along for a space without talking. After a time, Harker said, 'You are a strange one, boy. You look like a kid and yet I will allow that you acquitted yourself well back there. Did you really kill a man last night?'

'I did.'

'Don't it bother you none?'

'If it did, it would not raise him back to life again,' Tom pointed out.

'I killed my first man at about the same age as you are now,' said Harker. 'It was a funny thing. Like you, I did not worry overmuch about it after it had happened. Perhaps you are a natural killer.'

Tom scowled at that. 'I have no wish to kill anybody, but nor do I like being shoved around. If folk leave me be, I will do the same for them.'

Harker reined in and the two of them halted. 'What's to do?' asked Tom.

'Only this,' said Harker. 'I will help you get your sister free of those people. I said I would do it and I will. Howsoever, I do not engage to take part in a general war or anything like it. If you have it in mind to kill any of those who brought your sister into this mess, then I would be obliged were you to wait until you and me part company. Is that clear?'

'I only wish to get my sister. I do not seek vengeance.'

'That's probably a lie,' observed Harker. 'But so long as you don't do anything rash until I have left the scene, then it is nothing to me.'

It took them some time to find the house for which they were looking. When they saw it ahead of them though, there could be no doubt that it was the one that they were looking for. It was an imposing place and from a distance they could see that a lookout was posted on the rooftop.

When he saw this, Harker said, 'Hold up, son. Just stop now and look as though we have lost our way. Scratch your head and look puzzled.'

It took no great piece of acting on Tom Hogan's part to look puzzled at hearing these words. He looked at Harker in bewilderment, saying, 'I don't understand you, Mr Harker.'

'The case is simple enough,' replied the other. 'We are currently being observed from yonder rootop. There is a sentry watching us this minute. I want us to look like two lost, forlorn souls who have taken the wrong road. There now, let us go back the way we came.'

'I won't do anything of the sort!' cried Tom, 'I helped you as best I could and you engaged to aid me in turn.'

'And so I will boy, so I will. But we need to plan out what we are to do.'

Unwillingly, Tom rode back along the road with the Pinkertons agent. When they were out of sight of the house, Harker said, 'I am not going to ride against that house. It would be suicide. It is bigger than the one we lately entered and I can see that there are more than just two or three men there. Did you not see the horses in that field? Whether they have your sister held prisoner there, I cannot say, but I can tell you now that this is another of their manufactories for morphine. Most of the stuff is made up here, near to the Canadian border.'

'What do you want to do?'

'We will lure them into the open and then shoot them as they emerge. You are not against such an action?'

'Not a bit of it.'

'Here is what we will do. We will get close enough under cover to be able to take out their watchman. Then we shall make mischief and try to get them into the open, where we can pick them off with our rifles. Does that suit you well enough?'

'I reckon it will have to.'

The thing about making plans is that you often can't take into account what other folk are apt to do. So it was in that case. While Nathaniel Harker and Tom Hogan were discussing the best way to creep up on the men running the morphine factory and take them unawares, the lookout up on high, who was equipped with a powerful pair of army-issue field glasses, had already called down to his partners and apprised them of the state of play. Just as had been foreseen, as soon as the chemist and the other fellow had left the house that Harker and Tom had raided, they had come straight to the other base to warn those inside of what was afoot. They had both had a chance to study the two men who had smashed up the place and destroyed the morphine they had been making. When Tom and the Pinkertons man hove into view, even their very clothes had marked them out as being enemies on the prowl.

Harker insisted that he and Tom must leave their horses a good distance back from the house that they had it in mind to attack. Harker's plans included such scurvy tricks as getting into a good position and then shooting all the horses, who were loose in the field. He had an idea that this might be enough to draw the men out of their lair. He had yet to broach this scheme to the boy at his side, because he thought that the young man might scorn such a plan, tending as it did to the destruction of innocent live-stock. As it was, Harker did not get the opportunity to try out this ingenious plan.

Once the sentry had alerted those below to the presence in the area of the two men who had wrought such havoc at their other base, there was a general alarm and a call to arms. There were seven rough types in the house, regular bandits who would stick at nothing. They were hired on a cash basis and paid by the day to do whatever was needful to protect the interests of the boss. One of these men was the fellow who had been so effortlessly bested by Harker and the boy. In addition to these men, there were four girls, locked in a room of which the windows were barred. Also present was the little chemist and the manager of the Lucky Strike, a man called Northcote who was deep in the counsels of those who ran the whole morphine racket in that part of the country.

69

When word was called down that enemies were approaching the seven hired guns fetched rifles and took up positions on the side of the house facing the direction from which the riders had come. So it was that when Nathaniel Harker and Tom Hogan came dodging and crawling through the long grass that carpeted the land around the house, they were actually entering a trap. They fancied themselves the beaters, but in reality they were the quarry.

'Listen to me now, son,' said Harker, as the two of them crawled slowly and carefully through the grass, 'We need to draw out those men in the house. No good us just shooting at the walls and suchlike.'

'There is somewhat in that,' said Tom. 'What, then, do you suggest?'

'We make them come out by harming their interests. All those fellows have horses in that field. Leastways, I am guessing that that is what those mounts are, that is to say the personal horses of the men in the house.'

'Then what?' said Tom.

'We will shoot a couple of the horses and see what next chances, that is what. I'll warrant that they will come out to protect the remainder and engage us in fight. We will have the advantage, because we are in a hidden spot.'

There is no telling what Tom would have responded to this proposition, which was not a strictly honourable one. In the event he was not called upon to answer, because no sooner had Harker given his view than a heavy bullet tore open his skull, splashing the contents all over the grass, as though an over-ripe watermelon had exploded.

What had happened was that one of the men up in the house, over half a mile away, was equipped with a British-made Whitworth's sniper rifle, fitted with a telescopic sight. This weapon could be sighted up to 1,200 yards and was supremely accurate up to that distance. The blockade runners of the Confederacy had imported many of these weapons during the war and quite a number were still floating about in private hands. They were single-shot rifles and so, after killing Harker, the man who had shot him needed to go through all the rigmarole of reloading, which was lucky for Tom Hogan. If it had been a repeating rifle, then his little quest would like as not have ended right then.

As soon as Harker was killed Tom sensed what was afoot. He didn't know the full details, but of one thing he was perfectly sure; he was within range of the men in that house and they were aware of his presence. He did the only sensible thing that any man could have done, given his condition, and that was to jump up and run back the way he had come, jinking from side to side as he dashed for safety. As soon as he sprang up, a veritable fusillade of fire erupted from the house. At that range though, none of the rifles, apart from the Whitworth, was likely to have the necessary accuracy to hit even a stationary target, let alone one running and dodging as vigorously as young Tom.

He was out of breath by the time he reached the

trees where he and Harker had left their horses teth-
ered, but Tom did not calculate that he had any time
to spare. Once they had seen him fleeing for his life,
he figured, the men in that house would be saddling
up their mounts and taking after him. He turned
Harker's horse loose, mounted his own little pony
and made off back towards town.

There was no pursuit that Tom could see. Perhaps,
having dealt with the older man, those who had been
firing thought that they had neutralized the threat to
their operations. If so, mused Tom, then they were
fools as well as rogues. He was more determined than
ever to set free his sister and if that meant going up
against a hundred armed men, then so be it. But if it
came to such a pass, then he would make sure that
the contest was fought upon his own terms and not
those dictated by his adversaries.

Almost the first person he set eyes upon when
once he had got back to Confederate Gulch was the
Chinese boy whom he had spoken to near the Girl of
the Period. This boy recognized Tom and gestured to
him that he should come over. Tom did so, curiously,
and the boy said to him,

'Think about what you said. Very fond of own
sisters. I will help a little if you want.'

Tom was touched by this and said, 'Well now, that
is real good to hear. Can we go somewhere to talk?'

'Yes. Not here. Too many ears. You stay at hotel?'

Tom gave the name of the hotel and the boy said
that he would call by the place in an hour or so. This
would not put him in hazard, as he was always

running various errands for his uncle, which entailed his going into hotels and saloons. Tom was sorry about the Pinkertons man. He had conceived something of a liking for the fellow in the short time that they had known each other. Still and all, there was no manner of use in grieving for him. Doubtless he had known the risks of his job better than anybody.

It would be coming on evening soon and Tom was ravenously hungry. After returning the pony to the livery stable and intimating that he might need him again either that day or the next, he made his way to the hotel. When he got there, he ordered a meal to eat in the bar. He felt quite the man of the world, ordering a steak in a hotel like this. It was strange to consider how his life had changed so rapidly in such a short space of time since leaving home just a week ago.

The food was very welcome and he tucked into it with a good will. He was used to going without vittles from time to time, so he did not always feel hungry in the way that somebody used to regular and substantial meals might feel when called upon to miss a meal or two. After wolfing down the steak and potatoes, Tom found himself better able to concentrate his mind upon the next stage of the proceedings. He was about to get up and go to his room, when who should appear but Jane, the hurdy girl who had set him upon the right track to begin with. Tom rose and invited her to sit at his table.

'I guessed that such a big spender as you would make sure to choose a good hotel like this to stay in,' said the girl. 'It wasn't hard to track your path.'

'How can I help you?'

'I think that the boot is all upon the other foot. It is me as can help you. There is some men looking for you and they don't mean you any good neither.'

This was disturbing news. Could word of his actions at the morphine manufactories really have spread this quickly to Diamond City? Tom wondered if they had something like a telegraph line. Nothing else would explain the speed with which word of his and Harker's actions had reached town. He said, 'What men are these?'

'How can you ask? Are you that much in the way of shooting men that you cannot keep count of them? Did you really gun a man down because he brushed past you on the sidewalk?'

So that was it. It was nothing at all to do with his recent adventures. In one way this was a relief, but in another it complicated matters greatly. Tom said, 'What do these fellows say they will do if they find me?'

'Were I you, then I would not stay around to find out. I took to you, I would not like to see any ill befall you. Besides, you gave me something like a hundred dollars' worth of gold. I figure I owe you at least to let you know when you are in danger.'

'That's real nice of you. I mean that. Tell me now, where can I find these men who have a crow to pluck with me?'

'I heard them talking in the Lucky Strike, not an hour since. They did not name you, but I knew from

74

the description that it had to be you. I had best get back to work. The boss will skin me if I am not back soon.'

Tom reached out and clasped her hand in both of his. 'That was kind of you, Jane, to take the trouble to come and warn me. It will not be forgot.'

'Well, I don't expect that I shall see you again. You will leave Diamond City, I reckon?'

Tom looked surprised. 'No, I still have business here. First off though is where I must speak to those men who are angry with me.'

'Lord, don't you let on that I tipped you the wink. It would be more than my life was worth.'

The boy laughed at that. 'I won't say one word about you. I will give it ten minutes after you leave and then mosey on down to the Lucky Strike. Then if anybody has it in mind to start an argument with me, well I shall be there. I think that it is all a mare's nest.'

Jane stood up and said, 'You are unlike most boys of your age. I hope you do not come to harm.' Then she was gone.

Tom went up to his room and took the pistol from his holster. He emptied the charges from the chambers that had not been fired and then, using a scrap of cloth, cleaned thoroughly the whole cylinder, taking it off the spindle to do so. Then he charged five of the chambers, leaving an empty one beneath the hammer.

It was odd. He had not had a deal to do with handguns until being given this one, but he found that he knew instinctively the way of it, notwithstanding that most of his shooting had hitherto been with rifles and scatterguns, rather than pistols. The Navy Colt fitted well in his hand and he liked the balance of it.

Once he had fitted the little copper caps over the five nipples of the charged chambers he was ready to go. He slipped the gun into the holster and then drew it a couple of times, to make sure that it was coming out smoothly. Having assured himself that all was in order he left the hotel and walked slowly over towards the Lucky Strike.

CHAPTER 6

Tom was thinking hard as he walked through the streets of Diamond City. A week ago he had been no more than an ordinary farm boy of the type you could meet anywhere in Montana; grubbing out a living from hand to mouth, often not knowing for sure where the next meal was coming from. He had always had a good hand with rifles and shotguns and had never worried too much about killing living creatures but, until a short time since, he would never have dreamed of taking aim at a fellow being, let alone opening fire on such.

Yet despite all this, here he was now, still that seventeen-year-old farm boy, but now with a deadly weapon swinging at his side. He was a force to be reckoned with and he could not help but speculate what would happen were he to encounter those two rascally road agents who had robbed him of his pa's rifle. Well, if he did meet up with them again, then they had best look out, that was all! He was nobody's victim now.

It must not be thought that Tom had forgotten about his sister in the course of all this excitement; far from it. He had been slightly reassured to hear that she was probably safe in that house out in the wilds. At least she was not employed in some cathouse or similar and the worst that was likely to be happening was that she was becoming accustomed to taking something in the opium line. That was nothing: he was confident that once she was back home he and his mother could help her through such a thing, which sounded to him to be in the nature of an illness.

So caught up was he in these thoughts that Tom walked right past the Lucky Strike. Then he recollected himself and went back. He paused for a second or two at the door. Then he took a deep breath and entered the hurdy house, ready for any mischief that might cross his path.

The saloon was quiet enough, the night having not got going properly yet. Most of the girls were clustered together on one side of the hall, with only three or four couples dancing. There might have been a dozen men seated round tables and Tom straight away spotted the group who had seemingly taken it into their heads to brace him. Even had he not recognized two of them from the other night, they were nudging each other and staring at him from the moment that he walked into the room. As he made for the bar, two of the men stood up and walked across the room to block his path.

Two things struck Tom Hogan most powerfully about these men. The first was that they did not have the look of hard-bitten fighters. He had grown up among farmers and knew some pretty tough fellows, but these did not look as though they were accustomed to fighting and so on. They were neatly dressed and the guns that they wore were shiny and clean, like items which they were hoping to show off. The second point that he marked was that both men were the worse for wear through drink. They were not staggering about and falling over drunk, but they were nevertheless pretty well liquored up. There was an air of slow deliberation about them both, which was often the precursor to befuddlement and stupidity. Tom had seen any number of men in this condition on the streets of Cooper's Creek.

Really, Tom Hogan was not looking for any trouble that night. He had enough fish of his own to fry, without trying conclusions with a pair of drunken fools like this. Maybe, he thought, they have it in mind only to shove me around a little because I am not as old as they themselves. We shall see about that.

Tom stopped six or ten feet from the men who were blocking his way. He didn't say anything, but waited to see how they wanted to play it. One of the men said in a slightly slurred voice,

'Who are you staring at, you damned snot-nosed little bastard?'

'I ain't astaring at anything much,' said Tom

79

mildly, 'I was going for to buy a drink and I find that you fellows are keeping me from reaching the bar.'

Every eye in the house was upon the scene unfolding nigh to the bar. The couples dancing had cut their revels short and the three musicians had decided to halt their exertions for a space and were also watching with interest to see what would happen next.

'Are you sassing us, you little runt?' asked the other of the two men. 'You would not be well-advised to do so.'

'What is it you want with me?' asked Tom quietly.

'What do we want? What do we want? You forget about shooting a man? You ask what we want?'

Something that Tom later reflected upon was how much the behaviour of these two men was like youngsters in Cooper's Creek who were trying to spur themselves on to some aggression. They would talk big and hard, just like this, to work themselves into a fury, until their feelings overcame their common sense. It was strange to witness grown men doing the self-same thing in a life or death situation like this, with all parties armed with deadly weapons.

The barkeep said, 'Hey, come on you fellows. Why not have a drink on the house and forget all this?'

'Shut up,' said one of the men, 'unless you want to get crosswise to us as well.' The barkeep shut up. Those individuals who were directly behind either Tom Hogan or the two men who were challenging him, discreetly moved out of the way lest they fall

victims to any stray bullets, should a sanguinary con-
flict result from all the talk.

'Well,' said Tom, 'Here I am. Everybody can see
that I am minding my own affairs and not looking for
any sort of fight. Don't trouble me and I won't
trouble you.'

'Trouble you? I'll lay you in your grave for what
you did to my partner.' Having got himself into a suf-
ficiently agitated state, the man went for his gun.
Tom drew his piece, cocked it with his thumb as he
brought it up and then fired before his hand had
stopped moving. He could drill a sapling at twenty-
five yards and these oafs were less than ten feet away.
There was little chance of missing. The bullet took
the man right smack-bang in the middle of his chest.
His companion had not been so keen to fight, but
the unwritten rules for contests of this nature were
clear. His friend had drawn first and so anything Tom
did was in legitimate self defence. The echo of Tom's
first shot had not died down and the man just stood
there, not knowing what to do next. Tom shot him as
well.

There was utter silence for a few seconds after the
shooting. Tom Hogan walked over to the table where
the men had been sitting.

'We may well settle this now,' he said. 'Is anybody
else wanting to fight?' There was no reply. He hol-
stered his pistol and then went to the bar.

The barkeep had watched the unfolding drama in
astonishment, fully expecting that the young boy
would be slaughtered by the two older men. Tom

said to him in a loud voice,

'You saw that I did not start that. They drew down on me and their blood is upon their own heads, like it says in scripture.'

'Sure son, we all saw what happened. Don't worry, we all know that you was protecting yourself. They boys were liquored up and if it had not been you then I guess it would have been somebody else they went after.'

'I do not think that I will stay now and drink,' said Tom. 'I will bid you goodnight.'

There was something infinitely more intoxicating than hard liquor to judge by the looks he had from the hurdy girls as he left the saloon. He could tell that although they might view the average customer here as some species of fool, they were right impressed to see a young fellow like him shoot down two men, one after the other. Maybe he was little more than a boy, but by God he could hold his own when it came to this game.

The lives of the two men whom he had killed that evening weighed not in the least on Tom Hogan's conscience. That is often the way, that once one killing has been done those that follow are easier and don't signify nearly as much. Shooting the drunk in the street had been a turning point in Tom Hogan's life. Being jumped by the road agents had shaken him and set him in a frame of mind such that he would never again allow anybody to take liberties with him. The drunk whom he had killed had been the first person to cross him after that.

Although he was very far from realizing it, Tom was now well on the way to becoming a cold-blooded killer, however good his motives had been in setting out on this expedition in the first place.

He remembered with a start the arrangement that he had made with the Chinese boy to meet him at the hotel at which he was staying. Tom hurried along, hoping that he would get there in time. On this point he needn't have worried. The lad who had offered to help him was always burdened with various chores and generally running late. Tom had time to refresh himself and wash before there was a tap at his door.

'I don't think that I caught your name?' said Tom to the boy.

'Chinese names difficult for Americans. Chan will do.'

'Well, I'm called Tom and I am glad to know you, Chan. If you can help me out, you will be doing a good thing. I want no fighting or trouble. My only aim is to find my sister and take her home.'

'You know about opium buying?'

'I know all that I need. I am not trying to stop anything your family is mixed up in. You can buy and sell all the opium you want as far as I am concerned. Only help me to free my sister and you will never set eyes upon me again in the whole course of your life.'

'You ever smoke opium?' said Chan.

'No, I never did. I tried whiskey a few times, but I did not much take to it. Is opium anything like whiskey?'

Chan considered this idea and then said, 'Like and not like. People drink whiskey one day, two days and then not drink it. Too much opium and you cannot live without it. Very bad. Morphine even worse. Men and women taking morphine often, they cannot live without it. Do anything to get more. You understand?'

'I reckon that I do, Chan,' said Tom. 'Here's what's what with my sister. She is being held prisoner in one of those places that you and your family are sending the opium to. The villains there are giving her this stuff regular and in the end she will not be able to live without it. Then they hope to set her to work in a brothel. You know what that is?'

Chan's face darkened. 'Yes yes, brothel I know. Bad business. Other girls the same. My family do not like opium traffic, but life is hard for Chinaman in America and Canada. Nobody wants us for jobs, nobody wants us to live near them. We must do as we can.'

'I ain't blaming you, Chan. I guess it is like buying and selling liquor. It causes a mort of misery, but then folks want the stuff.'

The two boys sat for a minute or two, each of them having the notion that here was a fellow who would make a good friend. They did not put it so, even to their own selves, but that was without doubt the way of it. Under other circumstances they would most likely have taken to going fishing together, or just hanging around. As it was, the shared enterprise of freeing Tom's sister looked to be the only adventure that they were likely to share.

'What can I do?' asked Chan.

'You know that there are two houses, not far from here, where the opium is turned into morphine?'

'Yes, I know them. Go there with uncle.'

'Do you now?' said Tom. 'Could you take me with you? Get me into the bigger of them?'

Chan thought for a bit, then said, 'Dangerous. House full of very bad men. I only go inside once. Smell bad with smoke and whiskey.'

'If you couldn't get me inside, could you just get me close to the place, so that I could hide in a barn or something? They have a man setting watch on the roof. If they see me coming, then they will shoot, I think.'

Chan said, 'Yes, shoot anybody who come near. Very dangerous men.'

'Could you do it, Chan?'

'I take food up to houses. Sometimes food, some-times other things. Yes, I could take you near to house. After that though, on your own.'

'Yes,' said Tom, 'That's understood. I wouldn't want to put you in any danger.'

The Chinese boy flashed him a smile and said, 'Danger is like spice on food. Life without danger is like tasteless food.'

Tom smiled back at Chan. The two boys might have come from quite different backgrounds and races, but they were as alike as two peas in many ways.

It was agreed that the following evening Tom would meet up with his new friend outside town and that he would somehow contrive to hide in the cart that the Chinese boy would be driving out to the factory. Tom would simply have to come up with a plan before then for how best to proceed with getting Kathleen from the house. He felt a momentary chill at the idea that perhaps she wasn't there at all. But there were, at least as far as he had been able to find out, only the two houses. His sister had not been in the one that he and Harker had raided, so it was most likely that she was in the second of them.

He and Chan bade each other good night and Tom sensed that the other boy felt the same liking as he did himself. It was a pity that he had not met Chan under other conditions than these. It seemed to Tom that the Chinese boy would have made a lively and daring companion.

After Chan had gone Tom Hogan lay on the bed and tried to reason things out. The first thing he decided was that he had best make sure that his guns were in good order. After that he would try to come up with a way of getting into that house and releasing Kathleen. He closed his eyes in order to think more clearly without any distractions, and before he knew it was fast asleep.

Tom was jerked out of his slumbers by a soft but persistent tapping on the door to his room. He opened his eyes and knew instinctively that he had been asleep for hours. The tapping began again.

'Just a minute!' he called, then rolled off the bed and went over to open the door. When he did so he found to his surprise that Jane, the hurdy girl, was standing there. He gazed at her in uncouth amazement.

'Ain't you going to ask me in?' said the girl.

'You want to come in?' he asked stupidly.

'That is generally the way of it when I knock at a body's door,' Jane said tartly.

Tom moved to one side and gestured to her to enter the room. He still felt a little muzzy from having been asleep and could not imagine what the girl was doing here at, what *was* the hour?

He said, 'Say, isn't it kind of late? What is the time?'

'Oh, don't be such a cissy. Did your ma tell you to make sure that you got a proper night's sleep and get to your bed early?'

'No, really, what time is it?'

'Half two. Have you a drink anywhere?'

'Jane, what do you want? You could have got yourself a drink in the saloon. You work in a saloon. You didn't come here at this time of night to look for a glass of whiskey.'

The girl sat down on the bed and looked around the room in frank appraisal. What she saw seemed to meet with her approval, because she said, 'I don't often get to visit this hotel. It's nice. Nicer than most in this town, anyway.'

'You did not say what you wanted?' Tom reminded her.

'Well, nothing really. Except to tell you how grand you were tonight. I have never seen anything like it.'

'You mean that's the first shooting that has happened there?'

'Lord no, not a bit of it. Most of them though don't amount to much. There is a heap of shouting, some drunken fool pulls a gun and shoots out a mirror or something and then he is thrown out. You were different.'

Resisting the urge to ask Jane if it was all right for him to sit next to her on the bed, which would have been absurd, seeing that it was his bed and his room that he had paid for, Tom seated himself next to her and asked,

'How was it different?' He was young enough to be flattered at hearing a beautiful young thing like this tell him how impressive he had been.

Jane screwed up her face in a way that he found oddly endearing. It obviously showed that she was deeply in thought, because when she spoke again, it was slowly and hesitantly; not at all her usual way.

'There was no bluster or brag in you. Most men who start shooting, they carry on awful before they go for their guns. They shout and swear, spit and generally carry on like they have lost control of they selves. There wasn't none of that with you. You was as polite as could be, spoke soft and pleasant. I never heard any man in that house talk so nice when a fight was brewing.'

'I wasn't looking for a fight.'

'Yes you were! Don't tell me that. When I warned you what was in the wind, some men would have run a mile. I have known men dig up and leave town at five minutes' notice when they hear that a bunch of men are after them. You came in there tonight for no other reason than to brace those fellows and settle matters in your own favour.'

'There might be somewhat in that,' admitted Tom. 'Still and all, they did not have to draw on me. They started it.'

'That is how it looked to everybody.'

Tom looked at the girl in surprise. 'What do you mean, how it looked? That is what happened.'

Jane laughed. 'No it ain't. For all that you were quiet and polite, you knew that you were goading them on. I was watching you. After you shot the first one, that other, he stood there without a gun in his hand, not knowing what to do. You shot him down as well.'

All this talk had the effect of making Tom Hogan uncomfortable. He knew well enough what he had done, but did not like to hear it spoken of so lightly. He had not wanted to be distracted in his efforts to rescue Kathleen by having to look over his shoulder, wondering when the friends of the man he had shot in the street would jump him. He had made sure by turning up at the Lucky Strike that the confrontation took place at a time and place of his own choosing and that it worked out to his advantage. He already had a bit of a bad conscience about the second man he had gunned down in the hurdy house and did not need to be reminded of it.

'You have not yet told me why you came here,' he said once again.

'Hey, that's right. I didn't. Well, it's this,' said Jane and, taking his face between her hands, she kissed him full upon the lips. Tom was so taken aback that for a second he failed to respond. Then he reached up and touched her cheek.

CHAPTER 7

Next morning, Tom woke up and realized with a shock that Jane was still lying next to him in bed. He could scarcely believe that what had taken place a few hours before was not just a dream. But here was the young woman herself, large as life. He watched her as she slept. He could not help but wonder if she knew that it was the first time that he had lain with a woman. Could girls tell such things?

As he was wrestling with this perplexing problem, Jane opened her eyes and said, 'Good morning.'

'Good morning,' he said politely. 'I hope that you slept well?'

She burst into laughter and said, 'Lordy, did you ever hear the like? How did you sleep? Gauging by how quickly you went to sleep afterwards, I should think you must have had a good night's sleep.'

'Yes, I did. Thank you.'

'I never pegged you for the bashful type. What ails you now?'

For some reason that he could never afterwards

fathom, Tom blurted out, 'That was my first time. That is to say, the first time that I—'

'I get the idea,' said the girl, 'Well, you did real good for a beginner.' Then they both started laughing and before he knew it they had their arms around each other and were embracing. There was no telling where this might have led had there not been a knock on the door and a woman's voice calling 'Room service!' in a perfunctory way before opening the door and walking straight into the room. When the young woman saw Tom and Jane locked in an embrace she was quite taken aback and, mumbling a hasty apology, she backed out of the room again, blushing furiously.

The entry of the chambermaid somehow put their plans a little out of kilter and the two of them began to chat in the most natural way, which, thought Tom later, was odd under the circumstances.

'Tell me,' he asked, 'How did you come to work in a hurdy house?'

'That's no mystery,' said Jane. 'My pa died when I was little and Ma remarried. My step-pa, he wouldn't leave me alone, he was always catching me alone and trying to touch me and such. I told my ma, but she said I was a liar and that if it was true, then I must have been leading him on and acting like a slut. So one day I waited until I was alone with him and made sure to have a piece of lead pipe tucked away in my dress. Well, he started along his usual road and then I pulled out that length of piping and cracked him round the head with it. Then I lit out.'

'So where did you go?'

'I had a little handbill telling of the great opportunities to be had by pretty girls up here in Confederate Gulch. I found my way here and I have worked ever since at the Lucky Strike.'

'Do you miss your home or your mother?'

'Not I,' she said. ' 'Course, I soon began in on the other thing, soon after I started at the hurdy.'

'What other thing?' asked Tom.

'Whoring, of course.'

Tom nearly choked to hear her use such a bad word so lightly. He said, 'How can you bear to do that, let alone talk of it so? I don't understand.'

'What's to understand? I need money and men are happy to give me theirs. It's a business.'

Tom could not somehow tie in this kind, warm girl with the picture of a hard, heartless prostitute that she was trying to paint. He said, 'Can't you make enough at the hurdy-gurdy house without resorting to such?'

She appeared to take the question seriously and frowned as she thought about how best to answer him. She said, 'I don't see that it's a whole heap better, to speak plainly. There's nigh on as much takes place in that dance hall as you would see in a bedroom.'

'How's that?' Tom asked, horrified and fascinated at the same time.

'Some of them fellows, they will try to get you to do things there on the dance floor or under the tables. Boy, you have no idea. A lot of those prospectors, they have nuggets of gold with them and they will push them between your breasts and then try to get you to fiddle with them down their trousers, while you are sitting on their lap. I could tell you some funny stories like that.'

'I have some business tonight, but perhaps we can meet again?' said Tom.

The girl looked at him for a long moment, before saying, 'There was hell to pay yesterday, after you left.'

'What, you mean about those men I shot?'

'What – *them*?' said Jane. 'No, I don't mind that anybody cared a fig about that. It was what you might call a good clean fight and nobody was fussed. No, I mean after that.'

'Go on. Does this concern me?'

'You'd know that better than I would, maybe. One of the fellows came in from those houses that I told you about. You have not told anyone of what I said? I tell you now that it would go near to costing me my life were you to let on.'

'I have said nothing.'

'Anyways, the story is that there was some attempt made to rob one of the places of all the morphine that had been made there. It was not clear to me what had happened, other than two men had been killed dead.'

'Why are you telling me this?'

'To set you on your guard, you noodle. I can't think it chance that I tell you of the whereabouts of those houses one day and then next thing I hear is

where there has been shooting, killing and I don't
know what-all else going on at them.'

'Does anybody think I had aught to do with it?'
asked Tom thoughtfully.

'Not that I heard. Why would they?'

'You're not fixing to say anything?'

'I told you, I have put my own life at risk by setting
you on that trail. Lord, I am not going to open my
mouth.'

His face split into a huge smile. 'Well then,' said
Tom, 'I reckon we should have us some breakfast.'

Word had spread around Diamond City of the boy
who had shot and killed three men in the space of
twenty four hours. There was a sheriff in the town,
but he did not seem overly eager to look into the
matter. The way of it was that if witnesses all agreed
that a killing had been in self-defence, then the
sheriff would not go to too much trouble looking
into and investigating the affair. The most that the
law would do would be to take a statement or two and
make sure that it had been a genuine and fair fight,
rather than some assassination or ambush. The
prospectors and miners were a hot-headed and wild
bunch and killings were not uncommon. As long as
they were only shooting and knifing each other and
the fights were more or less fair, then the sheriff did
not feel the need to exert himself.

A consequence of all this was that the shy young
farm boy found himself to be something of a
celebrity that day. He noticed that the bar of the
hotel, where he intended to eat his breakfast, was

very crowded when he entered it with Jane, but little guessed that most of those present had come for no other reason than to catch a glimpse of him. Shootings and knifings were, as has been remarked, far from uncommon in Diamond City, but it was rare for one so young to kill three men in such a short space of time. It was this great interest which prompted Sheriff Parker to recollect his official position and interview the young man.

Tom and Jane had just finished eating when the sheriff arrived with a couple of deputies, prepared for the possibility that this cold-blooded killer would fight a bloody gun-battle rather than come and explain himself down at the office. As for Tom Hogan, he was astonished to see three heavily armed men, two of them with shotguns cradled in their arms, approaching the table where he sat. He stood up with instinctive courtesy, causing the sheriff and his deputies to recoil, as though anticipating a fusillade of fire from the young boy. Tom said, 'May I help you, gentlemen?'

'I have reason to believe that you were lately involved in three deaths. Is that so?' asked the sheriff, eyeing the pistol hanging at the boy's hip.

'Yes. Yes I was,' said Tom. 'But I was defending myself against armed men. I had no choice.'

'That is what I have heard,' admitted Sheriff Parker. 'Still, I would like you to come to the office and swear out a statement on it.'

'You mean right now?' asked the boy in surprise. 'We were only now finishing our breakfast.'

The sheriff and deputies, all three of whom were quite familiar with Tom Hogan's companion at table, stared at Jane in a such a way that she announced,

'Oh don't mind me. I have to get off anyway, Tom. Don't leave town without coming to find me.' She leaned over and planted a kiss on his cheek. Then she stood up, nodded saucily to the sheriff and his men, and left.

'Well, son,' said Parker, 'will you oblige us?'

'I suppose so,' said Tom. He left the hotel, accompanied by the lawmen. The procession through the streets to the sheriff's office garnered much attention from the loafers and passers-by in the streets. It was widely known that the young man had been set upon and provoked, drawing and firing his gun only after others had threatened to kill him. The good-looking boy was therefore the object of sympathy rather than condemnation.

Once they had reached the office and entered it, Sheriff Parker eased up a little on the act. He said to Tom, 'It's all right son, I have spoke to those who saw what happened. There is nothing for you to worry about, I know that you acted in defence of your own life. Still, three men have died and it is my duty to look into it.'

'What do you want from me, then?' asked Tom.

'How would it be if you was to write out an account of the happenings from your side? You *can* write?'

'Sure I can write,' said Tom indignantly. 'I bet I can write as well as you can.'

'That's nothing to the purpose. It is not me as has

shot down three men in a short space of time. By the by, how is that not one of the three was injured? Each was killed by only one bullet.'

'I guess that I don't like to waste powder and lead,' replied Tom.

Sheriff Parker gave the boy a cold look. 'Do not venture to make jokes here in my office, son. If nothing else, I can keep you here for weeks as a material witness, even if you are not charged with aught. How would that suit?'

Tom shrugged his shoulders.

'Well then, suppose you answer my question properly. This is the way of it. We have our fair share of shootings round here in Confederate Gulch. Mostly, the only casualties are pier glasses, windows and chandeliers. Even when men are firing at each other, they are often as drunk as fiddlers' bitches and don't hit anything. Those that do stop a ball are generally only wounded. You shot three men and with only three bullets you killed them all. I say again, how come? Are you a professional at this?'

Tom could not help but smile at such a question. 'Lord, no. I work on my ma's farm. I hardly ever touched a handgun until but a few days back. My shooting has been with rifles and such.'

There was something about this whole entire business that Sheriff Parker did not like. He could not precisely put his finger upon it, but he knew that there was mischief afoot. He said, 'May I look at that pistol of yours?' With considerable reluctance, Tom handed the weapon, grip first, to the sheriff.

Parker turned the gun over and examined it closely. 'This is not a new weapon. Do you mind telling me where you acquired it? Was it your pa's or something?'

'It was lent me.'

'There is something not quite right about you, young man. I cannot put my finger on it, but I have a nose for those that will cause me problems. You are one of them. Do you mind telling me what brings you to this part of the country?'

'I am travelling about a little. There is nothing more to it.'

Sheriff Parker looked long and hard at the youth sitting in front of him. He was not in general a gambling man, but he would have bet a hundred dollars right then that his path would cross this boy's again before too long.

After Tom had written out an entirely truthful and accurate account of the two shooting incidents and the sheriff had compared it with the statements that he had already taken, the business was concluded. Before sending him from the office Sheriff Parker thought it might be wholesome for the young man to hear his views and opinions upon recent events.

'Where I come from,' said Parker, 'we have a saying. Once is chance, twice is coincidence and three times is enemy action. You have been mixed up in two incidents and I don't see that I have much choice but to call them coincidental. Don't let me hear that you are at the heart of any more such affairs or I will be thinking that you are not the innocent boy that you represent yourself to be. Now be off with you.'

It was not yet ten in the morning and Tom Hogan had the whole day before him. He was not meeting Chan until the evening and so it came into his mind that he should make the most of being in an exciting place like Diamond City. So far he had been too tied up in his mission to give much thought to the pleasures of a large town like this, which was certainly very different from the sleepy little backwater of Cooper's Creek. He had plenty of money at his disposal, the whole day before him and he was a young man. Perhaps, he thought, he should set out to enjoy himself.

The people in Diamond City could be divided into two very different categories. First, there were the miners and prospectors who came to town for their provisions and other needs; secondly, there were those who furnished the goldminers with the necessities of their lives, which is to say: food, liquor, gambling and prostitutes.

On the whole it was the townspeople, who supplied services and goods to the prospectors and miners, who had the best of the deal. Those who lived by searching for gold and digging it out of the ground had a very relaxed attitude to the wealth that they acquired in this way. They spent money as freely as they collected it from the streams and hills of Confederate Gulch. It was common for a prospector to run out of money entirely and be forced to leave the district.

This did not happen though to the storekeepers and saloon owners. Somehow, the gold excavated from Confederate Gulch had a way of slipping through the fingers of those who worked so hard to get hold of it and then sticking to the men in town who were running all the commercial concerns.

None of this mattered overmuch to Tom Hogan, who had several hundred dollars and a day in which to spend some of the money. He was like a small child let loose at a fair.

The first attraction to which Tom gravitated was a gambling hall. He had already found that he had a natural facility at the faro table, and he wandered into a casino to try his luck again.

Although it was only morning the house into which Tom went had a fairly good crowd in it. Some of the men had been there all night, others had come as soon as they had slept and had breakfast. The establishment which he had chosen was like a big saloon, only with a dozen games of cards running at tables. The dealers and bankers changed regularly, but the Golden Nugget never closed; it was open twenty-four hours a day.

Straight away Tom found a game at which he could not really lose. In high-class gambling spots a new deck of cards is opened regularly. At the very least the pack is shuffled frequently between games. This was not happening in the Golden Nugget, either through negligence or the sheer tiredness of the dealers, some of whom worked twelve-hour shifts.

Tom found that he already knew one of the games being played, though under a different name. Here they called it *vingt-et-un*, which was French. The idea was to get as close to twenty-one as you could, by asking the dealer for cards one at a time. If you went over twenty-one you were bust and lost the stake.

After watching a few hands Tom knew the order of cards in the pack. He could not be quite sure, because as the discarded hands were collected up and placed on the bottom, the order sometimes got muddled up, but he had a pretty good notion of how the cards would run. The dealers here were a lot more careful about taking the gold for bets than had been those in the tent that he had visited on the edge of town. Here they had little scales at each table, where they weighed out an ounce at a time to make sure that nobody was short-changing the house.

On his first few hands Tom won eight ounces of gold, which worked out at around $200. At that point the dealer took it into his head to shuffle the pack, and so Tom withdrew for a while and watched the play until he had an idea of how the cards were running. Then he sat down again and after half an hour was ahead to the tune of twenty-four ounces: a little shy of $500. At this point he quit the game and went out into the sunny street to see what else Diamond City might have to offer.

Had Tom Hogan been in the vicinity of the sheriff's office at the time that he was taking his leave of the Golden Nugget the conversation taking place there would have interested him greatly. Three US marshals were sitting at their ease and pretty well telling Sheriff Parker what they would be doing in his jurisdiction, without seeking either his leave or blessing.

The oldest of the three, a grizzled army veteran called Loames, said, 'To be blunt, Parker, these characters have set up shop in your area because they know they will not be troubled overmuch by the law. We're here to set that right.'

'You're not suggesting that I am on the take, I hope?' said Parker, his wrath rising.

'You hope away,' said another of the marshals. 'We ain't answerable for your hopes. Fact is, we mean to hit those bastards good and hard tonight. You better hope,' he continued, with an emphasis on the word *hope*, 'You better hope that word does not leak out about our intentions, on account of where you are the only person in this town we have told of our intentions.'

Sheriff Parker thought that it was time to assert his own authority a little. He said, 'Let me see that warrant again.'

Loames handed him a folded sheet of paper, which directed Sheriff Parker, and also everybody involved in law enforcement in the state of Montana besides, to offer their help and assistance to Marshal Loames and his colleagues.

'More of my men will be arriving at intervals throughout the day,' said Loames. 'We do not want to give the impression of an army mustering or anything of that sort and so we will not be riding as a party until we assemble outside town at dusk.'

'What do you want from me and my deputies?' asked the sheriff.

'You can start by keeping your mouth shut about this to everybody, including – and I might even venture to say *especially* – to your deputies. I tell you once for all, if word of this raid reaches anybody, then you are answerable.'

'And all this is over a little bit of opium coming across the border from the north, is it? I don't see where it needs a dozen of you fellows to come riding down on us like I don't know what.'

'Don't you, though?' said the third marshal, who had not yet spoken, 'Then it's because President Johnson himself ordered this action. That good enough for you?'

'What it is, Parker,' said Marshal Loames in a less confrontational way, 'What it is, is that there is too much of this new opium-based drug floating around. Since the war ended more and more men, and not a few women too, have been fooling round with it. It is the very devil and we are the boys to put a halt to it. Do you know how many men are using this morphine?'

'I could not guess,' said Parker.

'Well then,' said Marshal Loames, 'it is the better part of half a million, if you can believe it. 'Most all of it is being made with opium coming into Vancouver and San Franciso, through the Chinatowns in those cities. Tonight we are going to close down two of the little factories turning it out and we will do so in such a way as to make damned sure that those involved in trafficking the stuff get the message. God help anybody who is in those places we will hit tonight, because if we receive the slightest resistance we will burn them to the ground.'

CHAPTER 8

Knowing nothing of the debate taking place in the sheriff's office, Tom Hogan was taking things pretty easy after winning $500 at cards. He was beginning to have the idea that this might become a way of life for him. He had a vision of himself gambling away the night at cards and shooting down anyone foolish enough to get crosswise to him. He was, after all, only seventeen.

As he walked the streets of Diamond City he was still musing about the best way to go about getting Kathleen from that house. He knew that the men in there were ruthless killers who had not hesitated to shoot the Pinkertons man. There was little doubt that they would serve him in just exactly the same way if they they had cause to suspect that he was opposing their interests.

So far his plan stretched no further than getting Chan to drive him up there while he was hidden in the back of the cart. He supposed that it might prove possible to jump out at some point near the house and then wait up until it got dark, but then what? He could hardly knock on the door, shoot every man Jack of them and then let his sister out. It was a puzzle to which he had yet to find the answer.

It was while he was walking along the sidewalk thinking only of gambling, murder, bloodshed and revenge, that he saw a small child, who could have been no more than three or four years of age, trotting across the road with no more concern than if she had been walking in her own yard. A stagecoach was thundering down upon her and various other carts and riders on horseback had not marked her at all. Without giving it a second thought, Tom dived into the roadway and scooped up the little girl in his arms, removing her from danger in the nick of time.

'Well, little britches,' he said, 'that was a close thing. Now what are you doing out on your own like this, hey? Where's your ma?'

At that moment, a worried-looking woman of about thirty came running up, almost crying with anxiety and vexation.

'Mary-Anne,' she said, 'What are you about? If not for this kind gentleman, you might have gone under the wheels of that stage.'

At the sound of her mother's cross voice, the child began to cry, so Tom hugged her close, saying, 'Don't you fret now, little one. Your ma is only vexed with you because she loves you.'

The woman watched in amazement as her daughter, usually the shyest of creatures, clung to this unknown young man as though she felt completely safe in his arms. She spoke in a milder tone, saying to Tom, 'You have a rare gift with children, sir. That one will not normally go within a mile of anybody she has not known all her life.'

Tom Hogan was embarrassed, feeling that there was something a little unmanly about being told that one was good with children. He had the urge to explain.

'Truth is, ma'am,' he said, 'I help out at the Sunday School back home and I always did get on well with little ones.'

'You need not feel ashamed of being loved by little children,' said the woman. 'I believe that they know who has a pure heart.'

Tom was getting more and more uncomfortable as this conversation progressed. Here he had been, plotting his bloody exploits and now here was this gentle-looking woman telling him that he had a pure heart!

'Well, ma'am,' he said, 'I had best hand back your child to you and be on my way.'

'Why, are you in a hurry?' asked the woman calmly. 'Are you meeting somebody?'

He did not like to say that he was eager to spend some gold on whatever pleasures the town might have to offer and which he had not yet discovered, so Tom merely said,

'No ma'am, not at all. I am just, as you might say, walking around.'

'It is nearly midday. Won't you come and break bread with us?'

'It's very kind of you—' Tom began, but the woman cut in right quick.

'It's not at all kind. You saved my daughter from injury and maybe death. I would be an ungrateful woman were I not to offer you some slight recompense.'

'Well then, thank you kindly. I would be pleased to share a meal with you.'

This was not precisely the sampling of what Diamond City had to offer that had been in Tom Hogan's mind when he left the sheriff's office, but he did not see his way clear to declining the woman's offer without appearing mighty ungracious.

He set the little girl on the sidewalk and was disconcerted when she promptly slipped her hand into his as though he were her brother or something of that nature. Her mother evidently saw nothing at all out of the ordinary about it and they walked along in this way, with the child looking up to him from time to time with a fond expression upon her face.

He presented an odd appearance to those who saw the little group. He was wearing the tooled, black leather gunbelt lent to him by the retired gunman and looked somewhat dangerous. Anything more incongruous than the sight of such a desperate character walking along hand in hand with a little girl would be hard to imagine.

As they walked along the child's mother introduced herself as Mrs Cartwright. She was dressed modestly and spoke in a very gentle and calm way.

Tom wondered if she was a preacher's wife or something. She had that kind, assured and competent air about her.

They walked down several side streets until they reached the Cartwright house. Her husband was a carpenter and attached to the house was a workshop. Mr Cartwright was standing at his ease, leaning upon a wagon wheel on which he had been working. It seemed to Tom that this man's eyes marked every detail about him, from the fact that he was walking hand in hand with his daughter to the gun hanging from his belt. There was something about the penetrating quality of Mr Cartwright's gaze that was a mite unnerving.

'Eli,' said Mrs Cartwright, 'this here is Tom and when little Mary-Anne ran into the road, he did not think of his own safety, but just ran out and saved her.'

To Tom's way of thinking, this was making far too much of a simple act that anybody might have done under similar circumstances, and he became a bit bashful, saying,

'It was nothing at all to speak of, sir. I just saw this little girl of yours in peril and picked her up. It is not worth mentioning.'

'Do you say so?' said Mr Cartwright. 'If my wife says that you did an uncommon thing, I must take her word for it.' He smiled warmly at Tom, having come to a decision about him, seemingly. 'You will share our meal?'

'Thank you, sir. I would be honoured.'

Throughout this exchange the little girl still clung trustingly to Tom's hand and the warmth of that tiny hand in his seemed to Tom, by a strange fancy, to be warming his very heart. He began to feel ashamed of the fantasies that had been swarming and multiplying in his mind before he met Mrs Cartwright and her child; those foolish dreams of being a famous gambler and gunfighter. In the presence of these good people, all that was just a lot of nonsense.

'Come into our house,' said Mr Cartwright. 'Mary-Anne, you let go of this young fellow's hand now and go on in with your ma.'

The little girl trotted obediently off to her mother and the two of them went into the house. The man looked long and searchingly at Tom again and said, 'You will not mind leaving that weapon in my workshop here? I will have no guns in my house.'

'No, no of course not, sir.' Tom unbuckled the gunbelt and handed it to Mr Cartwright, who took it gingerly and, holding it as though it were something unclean and perhaps likely to dirty his hands, carried it into the workshop and hung it on a hook on the wall.

This incident had a deep and profound effect on Tom. Over the last few days he had got into the way of thinking that there was something very grown-up and grand about firearms of that sort. This decent man obviously regarded them as distasteful things to be kept away from his family. Tom Hogan's daydreams of being a romantically bad fellow were further dented by seeing how a real man viewed such things.

The four of them sat down to a simple but filling meal. Before they began eating Mr Cartwright bowed his head and asked a blessing upon the food. While they ate, he and his wife asked about Tom's family and his life. He was at first minded to lie to them and spin some foolish tale, but knew instinctively that it would be wrong to deceive such good people. With considerable reluctance, he told them about his sister's misfortune and his plan to set her free.

Cartwright listened very carefully to what Tom said and then asked, 'Are you certain sure that your sister is in this house? Is it assured?'

'It seems likely, sir. I don't know what else I can do.'

'It would be a terrible thing to start a violent attack and then find that it was all in vain,' said Mr Cartwright. 'Do you not think that you should try and make sure of it first?' Then he said to little Mary-Anne, 'Go help you mother with the dishes, child.'

When he and Tom were alone at the table Cartwright said, 'I have heard of some killing done here lately. Are you this famous young fellow who shot the three men?'

Now a very strange thing happened at this point. Since the shootings Tom had been swaggering around, thinking himself no end of a dare-devil fellow for being able to snuff out lives with as little concern as he would extinguish a candle. Now, sitting face to face with this man, he had a sudden and horrifying vision of how all that might appear to a decent, God-fearing man. Rather than seeing pride in his deadly prowess, he was inexplicably overcome with shame. He said in a low voice,

'That is so, yes. It was me as shot those men.'

Mr Cartwright said nothing for a spell, just looked at Tom sadly. At last he said, 'It is a fearful thing to destroy the life of a fellow being. A fearful thing, young man.'

Tom said nothing.

'And this affair that you have in mind of rescuing your sister, that too is likely to end in the shedding of blood. Is it not so?'

'I guess.'

'No man can direct another's footsteps in this world. I would most earnestly counsel and advise you though, to turn aside from this path. Have you spoke to Sheriff Parker about this?'

It was a simple enough suggestion, but it struck Tom like a thunderbolt. So bound up had he been in taking the law into his own hands that it had truly not crossed his mind for a moment that the proper course of action might perhaps be to set the case before the authorities and see what they made of it.

'I see,' said Mr Cartwright, when Tom did not reply, 'that this is a novel scheme to you.' He smiled. 'You will not mind an older man tendering some advice to you?'

'No sir, I would be right grateful.'

'You are of an age when all this – guns and shooting and killing and all the rest of it, looks very exciting and manly. Am I right?'

'I suppose. . . .'

'I was like that once, you know.'

'You, sir?' asked Tom in surprise, 'I would not have thought it.'

'Why yes, I have killed men and gloried in my strength and ability to outfight others. It is all well and good when you are fighting with your fists in the schoolyard, but when grown men behave so with guns, it is a terrible thing, a terrible thing. By God's mercy, I was drawn out of that life, but do not think that I cannot see the attraction for a young fellow like you. You will be famous and all the men will step aside in fear when you approach, while the young women will swoon with admiration.'

So eerily close was all this to what young Tom had lately been dreaming of, that to his utter horror he found himself blushing crimson like a schoolgirl.

'Aye, aye,' said Cartwright, 'I know the way of it well enough. That's always how it starts, but it seldom ends there. At first you are a noble man righting wrong and going on errantry like a knight of old. But believe me, it ends in your becoming a bully and braggart. Don't do it son, I beseech you.'

Just then Mrs Cartwright and Mary-Anne came back into the room. The child had clutched in her hands a story book. She went up to Tom and held this out to him. Mrs Cartwright said, 'She wants you to read her a story, I am afraid. You have become a real favourite, I have never seen her be like this with anybody before, let alone a stranger.'

Tom took the book and then patted his lap. Without hesitating the little girl climbed up and settled herself comfortably. Tom began to read out loud.

After Mary-Anne had fallen asleep in his arms and been gently removed by her mother, Tom prepared to take his leave. When he returned the gunbelt to him, Mr Cartwright said,

'Think on what I have said. Sheriff Parker is not a bad fellow and will be the best one to deal with this. Don't go charging off with a gun in your hand and hatred in your heart.'

So moved was Tom by meeting the Cartwrights, that he directed his steps straight to the sheriff's office, determined to do the right thing.

Sheriff Parker was fuming mad. Diamond City and the whole of Confederate Gulch were in his jurisdiction and he did not take at all kindly to a bunch of marshals descending upon the area and laying down the law to him about what he could and couldn't do; even whom he could and couldn't tell about this. His two full-time deputies could sense that their boss was in a bad mood and were keeping their heads down and getting on with paperwork.

The door to the street opened and in walked the young man whom they had brought in earlier about the shootings. Parker looked up when Tom entered and said,

'What's this? Come to confess to more killings? I hope not, because you might recall what I warned you of earlier. Let me hear one word about another case of death by shooting in which you are mixed up and before God, I shall have you locked up.'

This was an unfortunate beginning. Being unable to cross the marshals with their warrant in any way, Sheriff Parker thought that he might as well take out his ill humour upon anybody else who could not hit back. Tom, for his part, was taken aback by this greeting, seeing as his attention was all law-abiding and aiming at doing the right thing. He persevered.

'I have come to ask for your help, Sheriff,' Tom said, as politely as could be. 'I am hoping to find my sister and free her. I have cause to think that she is being held prisoner near here.'

'The devil she is!' said Parker, astonished, 'Is this a new development? Why did you say nothing of this when you were here earlier?'

'I did not like to. . . .'

'Well then, son,' said Sheriff Parker, 'you sit down there and tell me how things stand.'

Tom related the story, leaving out some details, such as being in the company of the Pinkertons agent when he was killed. He finished by saying,

'So you see sir, I have reason to think that Kathleen, which is to say my sister, is being held prisoner in the house where this opium drug is being made.'

Parker and his deputies listened to this strange tale in amazement. The boy's voice had the ring of truth to it and they were none of them inclined to doubt what he was telling them.

'This is the damnedest thing,' said Parker. 'The damndest thing.'

'How's that?' asked Tom. 'Do you know somewhat

of this matter?'

'Never you mind what I know or don't know,' said the sheriff loftily. 'It's my business to know about things in and around Confederate Gulch. You would have done better to tell me all this earlier.'

'I'm telling you now,' said Tom.

'Don't get fresh with me,' said Sheriff Parker.

The deputies, who had heard vague rumours of drugs being brought across the border, were intrigued by this story and quite expected their boss to order them to saddle up so that they could all ride out this very minute to investigate these goings-on. Instead Parker said, 'Well, son, I am obliged to you for this information and you may be sure that we will act upon it in due course.'

'My sister is in danger right now,' said Tom. 'I don't know about due course, but from what I hear she is being given this poison regular, so that she will be fit for the purposes of those men. "Due course" is not enough, Sheriff. I have told you where she is. Will you act this day?'

Parker could not reveal what he knew of the raid that was planned that very day upon the house where this young fellow said his sister was being held captive. He feared to get crosswise to Marshal Loames and his men, who, he suspected, could make a heap of trouble for him if they were inclined to do so. He thought the best tack was to discourage this young boy and then later on pretend that he himself had arranged for the marshals to raid the isolated farmhouse.

Parker said, 'I will not be buffaloed and stampeded in this way. 'Specially not by a child who is barely out of diapers. I am the sheriff here and I will choose when to act and how to act and everything about the case. Is that clear?'

'You will do nothing this day?' asked Tom.

'I will not make you a party to my decisions. You have laid a complaint and now we will look into it in our own time. I advise you to go off and behave respectable and peaceably and you might hear more of this soon.'

Tom looked at the older man with contempt and the thought crossed his mind that perhaps the sheriff was corrupt and being bribed by those who were running the rackets in this town.

Maybe Parker guessed what the youth was thinking, because he said irritably, 'Go on, get out of here. I will not be crowded into doing anything.'

After Tom Hogan had left the office, the deputies looked at Sheriff Parker questioningly. He said to them, 'I will skin you boys alive if you breathe a word of it to anybody outside this office, but here is what is going on.'

It is always a frustrating and dispiriting experience when you have resolved to turn over a new leaf and do the right thing and then it does not turn out as you would have hoped. Tom Hogan left the sheriff's office feeling let down and sorrowed by the attitude that Parker had exhibited towards him. Well, he had tried. He had allowed the authorities a chance to take on the matter and as far as he was able to see, they had declined. He was still mindful of what Mr Cartwright had said to him, but he did not see that he had another choice now, but to go ahead with his original plan.

His conversation with Cartwright had had some good effect upon Tom, even if he was still about to undertake something in the gunfighting and killing line, and that was this: his half-hearted dreams of making a living as a gambler and carrying a gun all the time had evaporated like the morning dew. He was only a plain fellow from a farm. He had his ma to take care of and a sister too, when once she could be brought home. When he had brought this present matter to a satisfactory conclusion, then he and his sister would be heading back to Cooper's Creek and resuming their everyday life.

Back at his hotel room, Tom checked that he was altogether ready for the evening ahead of him. He was torn between regret that he had been unable to persuade Sheriff Parker to take action and exultation that he was about likely to have a lively time of it himself up at the farmhouse. There was still an hour or more before he was supposed to be meeting Chan and so he could see no better way of passing the time than by having a snooze. One way and another, he had not had much sleep last night and he wished to be sure that he was feeling fresh and alert for the trying time which surely lay ahead of him.

The three marshals who had lately been in the

sheriff's office were now esconced in a saloon. They were not getting drunk, but then again, neither were they remaining sober. None of them was wearing his badge and they were huddled over a small round table, with nobody on either side of them.

Loames said, 'I do not purpose to hazard our own lives in this endeavour, if you all apprehend my meaning.'

One of the other two, a man called Winterflood, said, 'I am all in favour of that. Hell, it ain't like we don't know what those bastards are up to there. We only want to set them as an example of what might happen to others engaged in trafficking this gear, ain't that right?'

'That's about the strength of it,' Loames agreed. 'I do not want the bother of being burdened with prisoners that we will have to cart around the country for who knows how long. We will deliver a sharp lesson to these types and hope that they get the message.'

The third of the men, who was a little slower on the uptake, said, 'You mean, then, we are not going to make any arrests tonight?'

The other two laughed indulgently. Jethro Pyke might not be the brightest soul in this world, but his meanness and toughness made up for this lack of brains.

'Jethro,' said Loames, aiming to make the case clear enough for anybody, 'we are going to kill everybody in that house and burn it to the ground. Is that plain? There will be no calling for surrender.'

Pyke's face split slowly into a grin. 'I get you boss.

Almost like this was pleasure and not duty.'

Loames laughed again. 'Yeah, you got that right, Jethro.'

CHAPTER 9

Chan was sitting in his uncle's house, listening to the conversation. Diamond City did not have a proper Chinatown, at least not in the way that Vancouver and San Francisco did. Instead, there were two or three streets in the town where by common consent anybody other than white, English-speaking Anglo-Saxons lived. There were Irish Catholics who had been labouring as navvies on the railroads, a few Mexicans, one or two black men, and three houses full of Chinese men most of whom worked either at running laundries or eating-houses.

Like any good Chinese young person, Chan was sitting quietly and respectfully, not interrupting his elders. The talk was of the difficulties and expense of bringing goods across the Pacific Ocean and then moving them from Vancouver to Montana. A certain delicacy prevented his uncle and the other man from actually naming the goods, but there was no doubt that it was opium about which they were talking.

Chan's family had interests in this trade going back centuries.

Until three years previously the amount of opium being run into Vancouver was minute. Not all Chinese smoked it and so enough was brought in to cater only for the more debauched types who haunted the opium dens down by the docks. When morphine was first synthesized in Europe in 1857 there was a surge in demand for the produce of the opium fields of Afghanistan and the Ottoman Empire, but since this was transported by way of the Mediterranean, this hardly affected Chan's family, who came from Hong Kong. It was during the Civil War that demand rocketed. Morphine proved to be the most effective painkiller the world had ever seen and the demand for it in time of war was unlimited. Chan's family became rich overnight.

Everybody thought that once the war ended the need for morphine would decline and it would become just another of those minor drugs which were used in hospitals for extreme cases. Nobody could have imagined that many of those men who were introduced to the morphine habit as a result of injury would acquire a passionate taste for it and be prepared to pay good money for it years after the war was over.

With over 500,000 regular users of morphine in the United States in 1868, the Chinese had pretty well cornered the illegal market in opium. It was brought into Canada and the United States and then converted to morphine in scores of makeshift laboratories, mainly

situated on or near the west coast. Chan's family supplied all the little factories of this sort in Montana and
he was gradually learning the trade.

'One laboratory completely destroyed,' said his
uncle to the other man. 'Everything smashed up. We
have five hundred pounds weight of the goods now
waiting just over the border. But the customers will
only want half of that now. We must keep the rest
under guard.'

'It is time to stop. The Canadians and the
Americans are both getting harsher about their
methods. We need not work again for many years
now. We all have enough money.'

Chan's uncle mulled over this proposition and
then said, 'The boy is taking food to the house
tonight. After that, no more. Tonight we finish for
good.'

Part of the art of being a good and honourable
young man was to appear attentive, but not too attentive. Chan had long ago mastered the art of looking
as though he were ready to jump up and obey
instructions, but also seeming not to hear what was
being spoken of, if that was preferred.

'Chan,' said his uncle, 'take the cart tonight.
Tomorrow we all get ready to leave. You understand?'

'Yes, Uncle.'

Having explained matters to his deputies, whom he
trusted better than he did his own wife not to go
blabbing about it, Sheriff Parker said to them,

'That's how it stands, boys. Those marshals have a

warrant that obliges us to offer them help if it's asked
for and otherwise to keep our noses out of things.
What they plan up at the old Stanton place is more
than I can tell you.'

'You think it's true what that boy says about his
sister being held up there?' asked Mike Clanton, one
of his deputies.

'Yes, like as not. Those hurdy girls are a skittish
bunch. If the boys running them houses could find a
way to tie the girls to them, why then I recokon they
would take to it. I have heard something about this
morphine racket and I dare say you two have as well.
Getting a girl into the habit would make sense.'

'Sheriff, if there are innocent girls being held up
at that house, I say we have a duty to go up there and
set them free.'

'My mind has been running along similar lines,'
admitted the sheriff, 'but it may not be as simple as
we might hope.'

'Meaning that there are like as not a dozen armed
men up there, who will think nothing of firing on
us?' asked the other deputy, whose name was Lane.
'How if we was to take the manager of the Lucky
Strike and also the fellow that runs the Girl of the
Period? If we rode up there with those two and told
them that we would exchange the girls for their
friends, then that might do the trick all right.'

Sheriff Parker's eyes lit up. 'You know, I think that
you might have it. That we could get the girls freed
without all the inconvenience, as it were, of a pro-
tracted gun battle.'

'Yes,' said Clanton, 'and the best part is this. We could tell them that in return we would not bother them for twenty four hours. They would think that they had a day to pack up and leave.'

'And then, shortly after we go,' said Parker, 'that mad bastard Loames and his boys will ride down on them and there will be bloody hell to pay. I like it. Yes, I like it very much. I do not take to the idea of those girls being caught up in a fight between those marshals and their enemies. They strike me as the kind to stick at nothing and who might not be too careful about casualties among the innocent. I would not like to see women caught in the crossfire.'

The three men gathered up a rifle apiece and set off for the the two saloons, aiming to return with the managers.

Tom woke with a start and looked out of the window in a panic, fearing that he had been asleep long enough to miss his assignation with Chan. The sun was still high in the sky, though. It could be no later than four or five. He pulled on his boots and went downstairs for a bite to eat before setting off.

At about the time that Tom Hogan was sitting down to eat, Marshal Loames was meeting with two groups of riders outside Diamond City. These men looked more like road agents or bandits than law enforcement officers. There were four men in one party and three in the other and none of them was wearing a badge or anything else that might distinguish or set him apart from any ordinary citizen.

They all of them had that grim, unsmiling aspect that one encounters in professional killers, whether they be regular soldiers or assassins. They were not men whom anybody would willingly cross if it could be avoided.

Loames said to the men, 'Enter the town in ones and twos. I do not want to see the appearance of a unified body of men travelling about. We will leave in the same fashion at twilight. Eat, drink and otherwise refresh yourselves and your mounts and then be ready to ride out soon after sunset.'

'Is there any booty likely from this job?' asked one of the men.

'I don't know,' said Loames. 'I do not think so.'

Loames sat there until he was satisfied that his men had dribbled into the town without drawing undue attention to themselves. Then he followed on into Diamond City and made his way to a general store. He dismounted and entered the shop.

'Good day to you sir,' said the clerk. 'How may I serve you?'

'I suppose you sell lamp oil?'

'Of course. Any particular grade?'

'Yes,' said Loames, 'the cheapest. I want two gallons. I need empty glass bottles too, with corks in them.'

'Certainly, certainly. We have all that, no problem at all. Would there be anything more?'

Loames said, 'I want some wicking, for lamps. You stock it?'

'Surely we do. How much?'

'I reckon ten foot of your widest should meet the case. You have the inch-and-a-half width?'

'That we do.'

'I am obliged to you.'

Chan was waiting with the cart in the spot that he and Tom had agreed. Tom never was so glad to see anybody in his life. He was afraid that things might miscarry and it pleased him that at least he could look forward to an hour or two's ride in the company of a boy who could almost be thought of as a friend.

'Hidy, Chan,' said Tom. 'I surely am glad to see you this day.'

'Get up quick, Tom. Uncle near by, not want him to see us.'

'Sure thing,' said Tom, and he hopped up on to the buckboard. Then the two boys set off north.

Looking back on that day with hindsight, it was possible to guess that something would go awry with Sheriff Parker and his deputies' plan for arresting the managers of the Lucky Strike and the Girl of the Period. These were men who were closely bound up in most of the rackets running in Confederate Gulch, whether involving gambling, prostitution or the trade in morphine. Word had spread about the destruction of one of the laboratories outside town and it was also known that a Pinkertons man had been killed near the other base. Everybody's nerves were on edge and there could hardly have been a more inopportune time to try and seize two of the men deep in these affairs.

Although it was common enough to hear shooting in Diamond City, none of it was ever directed against law officers. Parker and his two men had therefore no apprehension of danger when they marched into the Lucky Strike with rifles under their arms and demanded to speak to the man running the house. They were told that he was upstairs and could not see them at the moment, which did not please Sheriff Parker at all.

'That won't answer,' he said. 'Just you fetch him down this minute or we will go up and bring him down ourselves.'

The barkeep went off doubtfully and returned with the same message: Mr Northcote was engaged right now, but would be glad to stop by the office later.

'He'll be glad to stop by the office, hey?' said Parker wrathfully. 'He won't be so glad when I catch ahold of him, let me tell you that.' He turned to his two deputies. 'Come on, boys. Let's go and impress upon Mr Northcote most forcefully, that now is not the day for such shilly-shallying.'

In Northcote's room over the hurdy house was Northcote himself, Chan's uncle and three hired guns. The subject under discussion was whether or not Northcote was going to pay for all the opium waiting just over the border in Canada and if not, whether Chan's uncle would then feel free to sell it to another buyer. Things were getting pretty heated.

'You know damned well,' said Northcote, 'that we cannot handle the whole amount right now, not with one laboratory out of action. But we still want the stuff. Hold fire for a week or two, until we have another operation up and running.'

But Chan's uncle had no intention of waiting. He and his family had not become the successful merchants that they were without developing a sixth sense for danger. He knew that the free trade in opium was coming to an end and it was his intention to get out of the business while the going was good. If Northcote wouldn't buy the goods today and hand over cash, then he would sell them to whoever he could, even at a loss.

'No good wait,' he said. 'Money now or no goods. Simple.'

'I ain't about to allow a Chink to railroad me so—' began Northcote, when there came a sharp and authoritative knocking upon the door to his office. The person outside rattled the door handle a couple of times and then barked in a peremptory way,

'Open this door right now, you hear? Else we will bust it down.'

Now if Northcote and his cronies had been thinking quite straight they would have known at once that it was the law outside and that the best and most sensible dodge would be to unlock the door and let them in. Only thing was, tension was running high. Neither Northcote nor anybody else knew for sure what the game was. The raid on the laboratory could have been the law, but it could just as easily have been a rival outfit trying to close down their business. Such things had been known. So when somebody threatened to kick down the door, it could be the sheriff or it might be another gang about to charge in and cause them harm. All of which explains why instead of simply unlocking the door and seeing what was to do, one of Northocte's men drew his pistol and, before anybody could tell what he intended, fired twice at the door.

Mike Clanton, Parker's most trusted assistant and more senior of the two full-time deputies stopped one of the bullets, which struck him smack bang in the middle of his forehead. He staggered a bit, like he might have had too much to drink and then, right in front of Sheriff Parker's horrified gaze, dropped dead to the floor. This was the signal for a general bloodbath.

Although there were only the two shots, Parker and Lane conducted themselves as though they were under a veritable hail of fire and in peril of their lives. Parker booted the door, which caused the flimsy catch to burst asunder and the door to fly open. Parker and Lane then began blazing away indiscriminately with their repeating rifles at the half-dozen men in the room. Naturally, Northcote's hired guns perceived it as their duty to protect their boss, and so they returned fire at once. Thus a vigorous firefight began, with the two lawmen on the one side with their rifles and Northcote's men with revolvers. Northcote and Chan's uncle took no part in the affair.

By the time the shooting had died out, Sheriff Parker and his remaining deputy were dead, as were

Northcote and two of his men. Chan's uncle had had the presence of mind to hurl himself to the floor as soon as the battle started and so escaped without so much as a scratch. The surviving gunman had caught a bullet in the fleshy part of his upper arm, but did not fear it to be a serious wound.

As soon as this man realized that the opposition were all killed, he fled from the smoke-filled room at once. Chan's uncle also made himself scarce, not wishing to become involved in any awkward questions about what he had been doing there in the first place.

When some of the staff of the Lucky Strike ventured up the stairs, as soon as they were sure that the shooting had stopped, it was to find the aftermath of a massacre. Six men had been slain, three on either side. Mind, it was hard at first to be sure what had happened, because the thick smoke from all the shooting had created something akin to a fog up there. But when once the windows had been thrown open and the air began to circulate, it was possible to piece together what had occurred.

The people working at the Lucky Strike were appalled at this turn of events; less because of the senseless waste of human life than because the resulting investigations would almost certainly end in the closure of the house. There was not a man or woman working there who had not known that Northcote had been mixed up in an awful lot of dubious and unsavoury enterprises. A number of the girls cleared out that very night, being unwilling to face any questions about their own lives at the hurdy house.

While the aftermath of this shooting at Diamond City's most popular hurdy-gurdy house was being dealt with ten grim-faced men were assembling on the road leading north out of Confederate Gulch. Marshal Loames had slung all his recent purchases over the back of his horse in a pannier-like arrangement. Now that everybody was together he addressed them all and set out his vision for the expedition ahead of them.

'You men all know that we have been charged as federal officers with the task of closing down the trade in morphine. Some of our boys are targeting the Chinks and their damned opium trade. Pinkertons have been providing intelligence and also harrying some of the manufacturers and suppliers of this poison. Our job is a little different.'

'And you say there's no chance of looting anything on this one?' asked one of the men.

'Will you men just shut up about loot?' said Loames in a bad-tempered way. 'You are being paid right good wages. Booty and loot are all well and good when they come up, but they are not the purpose of what we are doing. Strikes me some of you fellows would do better setting up as bandits rather than US marshals.'

'So what's different about this job?' asked another of the men.

'If I can get my damned words out without one of you fools interrupting me, then I will tell you. We are going to make an example of this place. By which I mean we are going to kill all those we find there and then burn the house down. We will make such a massacre here that nobody as hears about it will dare to think about bringing opium into the country or setting up so as to manufacture morphine from it.'

'So we are not to be arresting anybody?'

'No,' said Loames, 'we are not. All that we are doing here is showing what might happen to those who are found fooling round with this stuff. Like I say, we are setting them an example.'

CHAPTER 10

Tom and Chan were having a pleasant time of it, for all that the purpose of the outing was such a grim one. The two boys were both thinking more and more, as they went along, what good friends they might have been under different circumstances.

'You ever go fishing, Chan?' asked Tom.

'Fishing? Yes, fishing with birds. Rare fun.'

'Fishing with birds? How's that?'

'Cormorant with ring round neck and string on foot. He dive for fish and then cannot swallow. We take fish from him.'

'You're kidding me?'

'No, no. True story. Very old way in China.'

'You weren't born here, then?'

'No. Only came last year. Uncle say to send me to school in America.'

'You go to school?'

'No. Uncle lie. He want boy for moving opium about. A boy looks less dangerous than grown man. People don't ask many questions when they see boy with horse and cart.'

'What will you do for the future?'

'Who knows?' said Chan gloomily. 'All change now. No more opium.'

'You mean that this opium smuggling is stopping?'

'Maybe not all families. My family stop now.'

The horse and cart bumped along the rode for a time, with neither of the boys speaking.

Then Chan said, 'What will you do when we reach house? You think about that yet?'

'Yes, I reckon I have. When we get within a half-mile of it I will hide under that cloth you have thrown over the food in the back there. Then I will slip off when we are nearly there, once the sentry has seen that it is you and that you are alone. There is a big barn, not far from the house. I will rest up there until nightfall.'

'Then what?'

Tom gave a boyish laugh. 'Ah, well now, Chan. That's the biggest question of all. What then?'

'You don't know what you will do next?' said Chan in amazement.

'Not exactly I don't, no. But I will trust to luck and hope that something turns up.'

Chan shook his head. 'Suppose what turns up is bad man with gun?'

'Yes,' said Tom, 'that is what you might call the weak point in all my plans.'

The eleven marshals of whom Loames was in overall charge were taking a different road to what the locals called 'the old Stanton place'. Chan was obliged to take his cart along the road, but the men on horseback wanted to arrive without being marked, so they were riding across country. These men had all held various other jobs before being sworn in as marshals and their past histories would in the main not have survived any close scrutiny. At different times in the past almost every one of them had been a soldier, barkeep, gambler, cowboy, bushwhacker or even a robber and thief. They were not, by nature, a law-abiding crew and had gravitated to law enforcement because at least it protected them to some extent from the risk of prison or hanging. Those who employed such men were aware of their shortcomings, but sometimes in rough and uncertain times, such men have their uses.

When the party reached a little wood, a few miles from their target, Loames desired them to rein in and dismount. There was some puzzled grumbling about this, but such was his reputation that this was muted and restricted to vague expressions of irritation, rather than curses directed at him personally.

When they were all down off their horses, Loames said, 'Any of you boys ever throw a Ketchum Grenade? During the war, I mean.'

'I throwed such,' said one of the men. 'They were heavy and if you was not careful, they would bounce back towards you.'

'Well,' said Loames, as he lifted the pannier from the back of his horse, 'we are going to use something similar today.'

Marshal Loames took one of the empty bottles and

began filling it with lamp oil from one of the two flagons. When the pint bottle was full he produced the coil of woven wick and cut off a length about a foot long with his knife. This he fed into the bottle and then wedged it in firmly with a cork.

'What in the hell are you doing?' asked somebody in a puzzled voice.

Loames looked up in amusement. 'What, you think I have taken leave of my senses? Not a bit of it. Now watch.'

The marshal stood up and reached into his coat pocket for a box of lucifers. In the meantime, of course, the lamp oil had been seeping up the wick, until it was pretty well saturated.

Near to them was an outcrop of rock, which split the little wood more or less in half. Loames struck a match and set light to the wick jutting out of the bottle of lamp oil. When he was sure that it was burning well, he tossed the bottle overhand at the rocks. It shattered, and in an instant a sheet of flame engulfed the nearest boulders. The other men watched this performance with curiosity.

'That is like to a grenade,' said Loames. 'As you will observe. Only instead of exploding with force, it spreads fire everywhere. Here is the way of it. If we was to stand off from that big stone farmhouse that we are attacking and simply fire our guns at it, then it would develop into a regular siege.'

There was a lot of nodding at this, along with grunts of assent. Although these men trusted Loames, there had been more than a few private doubts as to the way that he was conducting this present operation. Most of those present had had visions of the marshals engaging in a fruitless gun battle against a defended position and had been wondering where the advantage lay for them in such a situation. The battle could rage all the livelong night and the men in the stone house would like as not still be alive come the morning. Now, things were making sense.

Loames read something of this in their faces, which were illuminated in the flickering, sooty flames from the burning lamp oil.

'Ah, you fools thought I had gone soft in the head, did you? Figured that this would be like the Alamo, with us charging a fortified redoubt? You shoulda had more faith. No, we will wait until it is pitch dark. Then we will tiptoe up, light these bottles and then throw them at the windows and doors of the house. We are sure to set the whole house alight. Then we run off, or for those of you who were in the army, "stage a strategic retreat", and wait.'

'I get it,' said somebody. 'They will have to leave a burning house. Then when they do, we shoot them down like mangy dogs.'

'That's about the strength of it, boys,' said Loames, 'And those who thought that Marshal W.F. Loames had gone soft in the head and was leading his men on a snipe hunt can go hang.'

There was a good deal of laughter and good-natured chatter after this speech and the general view expressed was that that Loames was a real card.

They were pretty close to the farmhouse now and so Chan pulled up and halted. He said, 'Tom, I know you want to help your sister. But think first. No good to you or sister if you are killed.'

'I know that, Chan, and I am obliged for your concern. I don't see though that there is a choice.'

'You are sure that the sheriff will not come and see these men? Ask about sister?'

'No, I ain't sure, Chan. But I cannot rely upon it. Every second I leave my sister in that there house, those men are filling her full of that damned poison. No, I cannot wait on anybody. I must thank you now for helping me in this way. I would not have had a chance if not for you.'

The Chinese boy frowned. 'Not much of a chance, even with my help. What do they say? It is your funeral.'

Tom laughed. 'Lord, don't say so. See now, I will climb in the back here and cover myself up. Make sure you drive nice and slow, so that those men can recognize you. I will say goodbye now, Chan, because I do not want to make a great speech when I jump off near the barn.'

They shook hands firmly and both were convinced that they would never meet again.

The cart rumbled along the track and Tom peeped out through the cloth. He could see the house and on the roof there was a fellow watching their approach. He wriggled round carefully and slowly, until he could see the barn ahead of them. By a great mercy, it was on the other side of the track from the house. This meant that he would be shielded by the horse and cart when he leaped off and, with a bit of luck, neither the lookout on the roof nor anybody gazing from a window would see him. It was coming on to twilight as well, which would also help to obscure his movements.

In the event the whole thing went as smoothly as he could have hoped for. As they neared the barn Chan slowed right down and pretended to be having some difficulty with the reins. Tom took his cue from this and rolled off the back of the cart, then sprinted to the barn, bending low as he ran. There was nobody inside the barn, where there was a hayloft reached by a ladder. He climbed up and found himself surrounded by bales of hay. Best of all was where there was a little window which gave him a perfect view of the house.

Well, here he was. He had a brand-new repeating rifle and a pistol. He also had enough ammunition for both to keep him going for a while. All there was to do now was wait until it was completely dark and then go up to the house and see if he couldn't tackle those within.

Loames and his men were also idling away their time until it was pitch dark. There was desultory conversation about stunts that they had been mixed up in in the past. These men worked usually in different towns; different states too. But they could all get leave to join Loames when he sent out the call. It was widely known that W.F. Loames was a man that the government used from time to time when they wanted a thing done smart and efficiently, without too much fuss about the finer points of the law. He was given a task and then left to recruit whoever he thought might fit the bill.

Pinkertons had also been engaged by Washington to begin the fight-back against the opium and morphine scourge, which was, of course, how Nathaniel Harker had come to be scouting round the same area as Loames. Indeed, the two men had known each other slightly. The operation in Montana was one of several taking place along the west coast and the aim was to send out a stern warning to those trafficking in drugs. The message was a simple one: you are apt to get killed without a trial and this game is no longer worth the candle.

'You men had better come over here and fill yourselves a bottle each,' said Loames.

'How many of those bottles you got?' asked somebody.

'Enough for all of you to have at least one,' said Loames. 'Come on, look lively. It is nearly dark.'

'What's to do? Are we going to leave our horses some way off and tiptoe up on foot?'

'That's the way of it, yes. We will all then light our bottles and throw them through windows. Then we turn and run back.'

'I am not easy about a part of this,' said one of the men.

'Oh?' said Loames, in a voice which suggested that this was not the kind of conversation that he wanted to have right then. 'What are you not happy about?'

'It is one thing to kill all those fellows making the morphine, but what if there are others there? Girls or something?'

'You are in the wrong line of work, Catchpole,' said Loames contemptuously. 'With a delicate conscience like that, you might be better teaching Sunday School or running a mission.' There was a gale of laughter at this.

The man who had raised the objection said, 'Don't you set mind to my conscience, Loames. I am game for anything, but I just want to be sure that there are no innocent parties in that house.'

'You want to go and check, before we attack?' enquired Loames mockingly. 'You want to take the warrant and knock on the door? What the hell is wrong with you? We are making an example of these people, not issuing them with a summons for spitting on the sidewalk.'

Loames stood up and addressed the group. 'Listen, you men. We have instructions that come right from the White House. Here is the truth: we are directed in writing to raid this place and arrest those present. Howsoever, I have been told in person by somebody from the Department for the Interior that they do not want any long trials. Half those types will have slick lawyers and would get off. That won't discourage this trade. We have permission to use deadly force if they resist. Well, all I can tell you is that they look to me like they *will* resist.'

Catchpole did not say any more. He had heard a

rumour from a saloon girl that there were some hurdy girls being held up at this house. The details were vague, but he really had felt a twinge in his conscience about this. It was not sufficient, though, to cause him to stand up against Loames and everybody else and so he let the matter rest.

In the barn Tom was turning over in his mind what had happened in the last week or two. He had killed a man – well, three to be accurate – and also laid with a woman for the first time. Like for any boy of his age, these were mighty exciting events; to say nothing of his being a successful gambler.

It was not upon those things that his thoughts were focused, though. He was thinking instead of the Cartwrights. Mr Cartwright, that steady, sober individual with such a strong way about him; his wife, so gentle and kind; and of course the little girl.

Tom found that two images had been contending for mastery in his thoughts. One was of a tough man who gambled in saloons and shot down his enemies mercilessly; the sort of man whom everybody feared and respected; a fellow whom girls would be looking at with longing in their eyes. Although he had never considered the question too deeply, he realized that this was always what he had assumed it meant to be a man. To be strong and not let anybody push you around. But Mr Cartwright was not a bit like that. Here was a fellow who looked after his wife and child and set the care of his family above all else. A man who regarded guns as being dirty things, such as he would not want in his house.

It came to Tom that when it came down to it he would sooner feel the soft, trusting hand of a small child in his than he would the smooth, cold and deadly grips of a pistol. He felt sure that he had taken a wrong turn since coming to Confederate Gulch and he wondered if it would not suit his disposition a whole lot better to make a good man like Mr Cartwright his pattern, rather than some of the men whom he had encountered since his arrival.

It was quite dark now and Tom did not believe that he had any more excuse for delay. He did not much want to start any shooting and the dream that had taken root in his spirit of one day having a wife like Mrs Cartwright and little ones of his own was undiminished, but when all the arguments had been made, his sister was still held prisoner in that house by a set of rascals. He did not believe that he would be any sort of a man in the future if he left her to her fate. This present affair was quite different from the gambling and the shooting of strangers because they crossed him. This was an honourable business and he did not know but that he would ever be able to look at himself in the mirror again if he walked off now and left Kathleen in such a fix. Tom checked that the rifle was cocked and stood up, ready to move in on that farmhouse.

Loames and his men were looking down a gentle slope, at the bottom of which was the Stanton place. Lamps were lit and it was fairly plain that there were plenty of folks at home. Lights showed in every window and although it was nearly a mile away, they could hear, across the still night air, laughter and shouting. It all sounded familiar enough. It was the noise of the bunkhouse or of the saloon; of a bunch of single men relaxing and enjoying themselves. There were, from the racket, maybe a dozen men whooping it up in the house.

'Listen up now,' said Loames, speaking quietly, even though they were a good distance from their target. 'We will leave the horses here. Those trees yonder will do as a base. Have you all a box of lucifers?'

There were murmurs of assent.

'Then each one of you take with you your rifles and the bottles. We will none of us speak again before we reach the farmhouse. I do not think that they will have sentries posted. Sounds to me like they are having something of a party there. When we get right up close, I will raise my arm and you will all light your bottles. We will spread out and each man must mark his target, which will be a window on the ground floor. Then when I let my arm fall, you will all throw your bottles through the windows. As soon as you have done so, run like the devil and take shelter behind those low stone walls that you see running nigh to the house at about fifty yards or so.'

One of the men said, 'What then?'

'What then?' said Loames, exasperated. 'What then? Well you can play with yourself or something, you stupid bastard. What then? We fire at will, and kill every mother's son of them as runs from the house. With ten of these firebombs going in at once,

146

I don't believe that they will be able to put out all the flames before the fire catches hold.'

The ten riders walked to the trees that Loames had indicated and secured their mounts there. Then, in dead silence, they began walking down the slope towards the house.

CHAPTER 11

From the little window in the hayloft Tom could see that the men in the farmhouse looked to be having a good time of it. In the other farm, the one that he and the Pinkertons agent had visited, the storm shutters had been fastened over the windows, but there was none of that here, except only on two windows on the second floor. Tom wondered if that was where their laboratory was.

As he watched he became aware of something odd. Up behind the house was a rise of ground and silhouetted against the sky there were a number of figures. At first he thought, in the uncertain light of dusk, that they were bushes or trees, but then he saw that they were moving down the slope towards the house. Maybe this was Sheriff Parker and a posse, come to rescue his sister. It seemed to Tom that the best thing he could do would be to wait up in that hayloft until he saw how things were going to move.

Loames and his men walked slowly down to the house, all anxiously scanning the buildings and walls ahead for any sign of a lookout or sentry. There was none that they could see. When they were twenty yards away Loames raised his arm, the signal for everybody to light the wicks on their firebombs. Once he could see that all the bottles were lit Loames pointed wordlessly at the house and began to advance himself.

To anybody watching it might have looked as though the ten men were playing some children's game, such as 'grandmother's footsteps'. They crept forward on tippytoes, wanting to be quite sure that their attack came as an absolute surprise to those in the house. Through the windows they could see men milling about, laughing and drinking without a care in the world. It almost looked like some kind of party was taking place. Once he judged that they were close enough Loames raised his arm and brought it down sharply, as though he were swinging an axe.

The men all hurled their bottles through the windows. Two of them were extinguished by the act of throwing, but the other eight either shattered when they landed inside the house or the corks were dislodged, sending burning lamp oil over rugs and wooden floorboards. As soon as they had hurled the firebombs, all the men in Loames's assault party retreated swiftly and took up firing positions behind the low stone walls which connected old pigpens and hen houses.

Had the men in the house reacted sensibly at once it is possible that they might have saved themselves. As it was, some rushed at once to the windows, to peer out and see who had launched this attack. Others began beating out the flames, which were spreading up drapes and starting to engulf furniture. This served only to spread the oil about even further. What was really needed was water, but the only water in that house was that which was drawn from the well outside. The occupants of the house were not great ones for drinking water, nor using it to wash either, if truth be told. There was only one half-empty bucket in the kitchen, which was fetched and used to put out a section of wooden flooring which had taken fire. Another man, befuddled by drink, took it into his head that any liquid would do to extinguish the flames and he began pouring the contents of a brandy bottle on one of the fires, which caused the flames to leap higher than before.

Although Loames had at first told his boys to hold fire until the enemy came running out of the house, the sight of some of those men standing near the windows with the flames behind them was just too good to ignore. Several of the marshals began firing, accounting for three of the men in the house. Those who had been trying to beat out the flames now realized that they were making themselves into tempting targets by doing so. They dropped to the floor and allowed the fires to rage unchecked.

Up in the hayloft Tom Hogan stared in utter amazement at the spectacle unfolding below him. He had fully expected the shadowy figures to challenge those in the farmhouse to surrender. When the blazing bottles were thrown through the windows he had been unable to accept the evidence of his senses. It was when he saw the lower floor of the building becoming engulfed in flames and heard the crackle of rifle fire that he knew that things were just exactly as they appeared to be. Whoever was in the party that had been approaching the house had nothing other in mind than killing everybody in the building.

He watched as a door opened and a man called out, 'Don't shoot, I'm surrendering!' Somebody walked slowly out with his hands held high and was instantly cut down in a hail of gunfire.

From Loames's point of view everything was proceeding as he had planned. The house was blazing merrily and none of those within were able to take effective action against the fire. One man had run out of the house, making for the well, presumably to draw water to put out the flames. He died before he could even lay a hand upon the windlass. The marshals took pot shots at anybody who stood up in the rooms where the fire had taken hold.

Loames tried to guess what he would do were he in the house and figured that he would perhaps retreat up the stairs and hope that the fire died down. The surviving men in the old farmhouse had seen what happened to anybody who left the building and so there would most likely be no further attempts at surrender. They must know by now that his aim was to kill the lot of them without showing any quarter.

If he did nothing, then his sister would burn alive; Tom realized that all right. He whirled round and leaped to the ladder. As he scrambled to get down it, one rung gave way and he found himself pitched headlong into the blackness. He could not see to know when he was about to strike the floor of the barn. There was no pain, merely a bright light which flared briefly in his skull, then he was was engulfed in darkness and knew nothing more.

Precisely as Loames had guessed they would, the five men who had not been killed so far made their way up the stairs to where the laboratory was, and also the room where the four young women were being held. It was a desperate last throw, but it might, they thought, be worth appealing to the chivalry of the men besieging the house. They unlocked the door of the room that held the girls and ushered them out.

One of the men in the house shouted from a window that he had managed to open without exposing himself to the withering fire that still raked the house every time those below caught a glimpse of movement.

This man called out, 'You down there! It is not only us men here. There are girls up here as well. Hold fire and I will get one of them to talk to you.' A girl was forced to the window at gunpoint.

'Help us,' she shouted. 'There are four of us girls here. Will you let us come out?'

Loames shouted back, 'You girls can come out. Any men with you had best expect no mercy.'

The tragedy had reached its final act, because even if they had been given an offer of safe passage, it was too late for the men upstairs in the house. The staircase itself was ablaze by now and there was no way for them to retreat. They began firing out of the windows, down to where they supposed the attackers to be hiding. All the time the flames were taking a stronger hold.

When he came to Tom hardly knew at first where he was. It was pitch dark and for a moment he thought that he must be in bed and have woken after a particularly unpleasant dream. It had been something about Kathleen and a house afire. Then he recalled the whole thing in a rush and jumped to his feet. He ran out of the barn, then stopped dead in his tracks as though he had run into a wall.

The moon had risen high in the night sky and the scene was illuminated almost as brightly as it would have been in broad daylight. The farmhouse was a smouldering ruin; there was no sign of the men who had reduced it to this state. It was not the sight that caused Tom the pain he felt, although as God he knew, that was bad enough. It was the smell. He had been to a barbecue once, where a whole pig had been roasted over an open fire. The smell that now assailed his nostrils was similar to that, only a hundred times worse. When he realized that he was smelling the burnt remains of many people who had been alive a few hours earlier, it was bad enough. But he thought about his sister and knew that part of that ghastly stench was caused by his beloved Kathleen's body being rendered down to fat and charred bone by the intense heat from the burning of the house.

He began retching and then vomiting until his stomach was quite empty.

It took Tom almost four hours to walk back to Diamond City. He reached the outskirts of the town just as dawn was breaking. He had lost his rifle in the barn and had not bothered to return to look for it. All that he could think of was that he had failed his sister. She was dead, and such a death too! Burned alive. As he had trudged wearily along the road to town, Tom had cried several times both with grief and also with sheer vexation that he had been able to do nothing to protect her when it came down to it. He had failed utterly.

The night watchman at the hotel where he was staying was surprised to see him and looked askance at his appearance. Still, it was not his job to criticize how guests chose to look and dress.

He said to Tom, 'A young . . . lady came by, sir, and left this note for you.' He handed a piece of paper to Tom and waited for the customary tip. It was not forthcoming; the young man ignored him and simply walked right on, heading up to his room.

When he was in his room Tom lit the lamp; although the sun was just up the room was still gloomy and dark. He looked at the folded sheet of paper. Who on earth could have been leaving him a message here? He almost did not bother to read it. What did anything matter now, now that his sister was dead? In the end, he unfolded the note and read it. The handwriting was childish and ill-formed. He glanced down the page to see who it was from and saw that it had been signed, 'Jane'.

Dear Tom

I bet you are surprised to get a letter from me. I met a friend who was at the Girl of the Period and now works for herself. I asked after your sister and she laughed when I told her that it was feared that she had become a morphine taker. Nothing of the sort, she said. Kathleen stayed for a month at the hurdy and did not take to it. She lit out and said that she was going home.

I am sorry that I set you on the wrong track by telling you about those girls being held prisoner and it looks like your sister was not in the case at all. I liked being with you, Tom and hope to see you soon.

Jane.

He sat on the bed reading this. When he had finished he went over and opened the window. Never had the morning air smelled so sweet. So after all this, it was all fine. With a little luck Kathleen should be home by now, and all that remained was for him to follow on and make tracks back to Cooper's Creek as fast as he was able.

He was too excited to sleep and so after splashing a little cold water on his face he went down and had breakfast. The conversation was all about the death of Sheriff Parker and the big gunfight at the Lucky

155

Strike. It seemed that things had been every bit as lively in Diamond City as they had been out at the farmhouse that had been burned down.

There were one or two things that Tom wanted to do before leaving town. First off was a visit to the Cartwrights. Before he went he visited a store which sold a few toys and other goods aimed at children. Tom bought the best doll that he could find and carried it along of him through the streets, oblivious of the ridiculous spectacle that he presented to passers by. He reckoned that he had proved his manhood lately and that if anybody wanted to see him as soft or unmanly, well then, they would have to do so.

When he reached the Cartwright house Tom opened the gate and went to the workshop, where Mr Cartwright was planing a plank of wood.

He smiled warmly at Tom and said, 'I mind that that is not your own doll you are carrying around with you?'

'No, sir. If you will allow me, I should like to give it to your daughter.'

'I never heard anything so kind in my life,' said Cartwright, taking off his apron. Unbidden, Tom removed the gunbelt that he was wearing and hung it up. The two of them entered the house.

Mary-Ann was pleased to see Tom and thoroughly overawed at the doll, which he presented to her. The Cartwrights asked him to stay for a space, but he explained that he was anxious now to get back to his home and make sure that his sister really had arrived back there safely.

When he went back to the workshop with Mr Cartwright to pick up his gun, Tom said, 'I wanted to tell you sir, before I left, that seeing you and your family gave me a new idea about myself. I thought that I would one day like to have a wife and child of my own and live as you do.'

Cartwright put his hand on the boy's shoulder and said, 'Well, I make no doubt that you will do so one day. If anything you have seen or heard here has turned you from a life which includes shooting and gambling, then I am thankful that we have been of some help to you. Be sure to come by our house if ever you are in Diamond City again.'

There was now nothing to keep Tom from leaving Confederate Gulch that very day. He accordingly went back to the hotel and collected the winnings from the card games, which he had left secreted in his room. He decided not to try and track down Jane to bid her farewell. Instead, he went to the livery stable and engaged to buy the pony that he had previously hired.

After a little stiff bargaining he succeeded in fixing a good price both for the horse and the tack to go with him. After picking up some provisions Tom rode out with no further delay.

There was one final task to be accomplished before he went back home and that was to return the gunbelt and pistol to Caleb Walker. That individual was pleased to see Tom and showed great interest in all that he told him. He said to Tom that it was like a regular breath of fresh air to hear of his pistol being used to shoot somebody, which Tom found an odd outlook.

It was of curious interest to Tom Hogan to compare in his own mind Caleb Walker and Mr Cartwright. Both were evidently men who had lived tough and adventurous lives when young, but whereas Mr Cartwright had rejected all his former actions as being the folly of youth, Caleb Walker still hankered after shooting and killing and gained pleasure from hearing of such things at second hand. Tom liked Walker greatly and was grateful to him for his help, but on balance it was Mr Cartwright who seemed to him to have the better attitude to such matters as bloodshed and violence.

All things considered, Tom Hogan was mightily relieved to get back to the vicinity of Cooper's Creek without any more adventures or mishaps. His own view of the case was that he had had enough excitement over the course of a couple of weeks to last him for a good long while.

He felt a thrill of pleasure when his own home came into view and he found tears coming to his eyes when he saw two figures at work outside the house, hanging out washing.

'You took your time getting back,' was Kathleen's greeting as he rode up. Then she burst into tears as he jumped down from the pony and embraced her.

'Well,' said their mother, 'I do not think there is a

happier being in this world than me, this day.'

'You have even more cause to be happy than you know of,' Tom told her, before revealing that he had returned with some hundreds of dollars' worth of gold. At the very least they would not be on short commons for the coming year or so.

'You do not intend to gamble as a regular practice, I hope?' his mother enquired anxiously. 'I never heard of such a habit leading to happiness.'

'I do not look ever to gamble a cent again in the whole course of my life,' said Tom. 'Although the thought did come to me that I should be able to live through play at cards. I mind, though, that there are more important things in life than having easy money.'

Tom having delivered which thought, the three of them went into the house to prepare their evening meal.